'And what other secrets have you been hiding from me, Miss Martyn-Browne?'

For a moment her heart seemed to stand still, then it was racing hectically. But, with an effort, she forced herself to answer lightly. 'So many I don't know where to begin.' It was a relief to see him smile, and she felt she could hurry on.

'You know, you are very trusting, Jake. You have only my word that I am who I say I am. I could be perpetrating the most enormous con trick.'

'I'll lock my door tonight as a precaution.' Now his look was teasing but with a hint of a challenge.

'I promise you are quite, quite safe.'

'You disappoint me.'

Ginny found herself manoeuvred against the bole of one of the ancient oaks, and as he spoke in that low disturbing voice he placed one hand flat against the trunk, and hooked the other against her waist, pulling her into the curve of his body, effectively overpowering her.

'Jake.' It was a gasp of fear and longing. 'Jake don't.'

And gently, gently, all his attention on her mouth, he lowered his mouth to hers.

Alexandra Scott was born in Scotland and lived there until she met her husband, who was serving in the British army, and there followed twenty-five years of travel in the Far East and Western Europe. They then settled in North Yorkshire, and, encouraged—forcefully—by her husband, she began writing the first of some fifty romantic novels which were to be published. Her other interests include gardening and embroidery, and she enjoys the company of her family.

Recent titles by the same author:

DESERT WEDDING

A RECKLESS
AFFAIR

BY
ALEXANDRA SCOTT

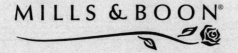

MILLS & BOON®

*First published in Great Britain 1997
Harlequin Mills & Boon Limited,
Eton House, 18-24 Paradise Road, Richmond, Surrey TW9 1SR*

© Alexandra Scott 1997

ISBN 0 263 80369 4

*Set in Times Roman 11 on 12 pt.
02-9709-47957 C1*

*Printed and bound in Great Britain
by Mackays of Chatham PLC, Chatham*

CHAPTER ONE

GINNY MARTYN-BROWNE paused for a mere second beside the enormous plate glass windows, scarcely aware of her reflection in that instant and moving on before she could be intimidated and turn tail. For the hundredth time since leaving Heathrow she questioned the logic of what she was doing—the morality, even. There was little doubt that her actions placed the happiness of other people in jeopardy but she had come too far, suffered too long, to consider turning back now.

HUGO VANBRUGH ASSOCIATES. Directly in front of her eyes, embossed in gold on the smoked plate glass, it was enough to intimidate the most supremely confident, and to Ginny, with her toe on the second or third rung of the legal ladder, it caused a distinct tremor in the pit of her stomach… Nevertheless she straightened her spine, averted her gaze from the crushing superiority of the gold lettering and refused to be deflected from her purpose—not at this late stage, when she had just arrived in the Big Apple. Perhaps a few days ago, before she had made her impulsive decision would have been the time for second thoughts, but now…

Now was a moment for a final check on her appearance, and the dark glass was ideal for that purpose. Not too bad, in spite of her fatigue—the hasty shower back at her hotel had helped to hold that at bay...

Hmm. The business trip to Paris last month had not been entirely wasted. The exorbitantly priced, sleekly fitted trousers had been worth every sou, their burnt-cream colour blending perfectly with the multi-coloured silk of her blouse and simple dark waistcoat. Make-up was freshly applied and understated. She was pleased with herself, and with the confidence she found to sweep past the uniformed doorkeeper.

She gave a flash of her business card and declared, 'Miss Virginia Martyn-Browne of Brockway and Laffan, London, to see Mr Hugo Vanbrugh.' Amazing what a little fabrication and a super-confident manner could achieve.

A moment later she'd been taken into the lift, and she stood there, heart hammering, palms damp while the attendant pressed buttons and they were whisked upwards.

She made an effort to divert her thoughts from the immediate, stomach-churning future. At least now she could return to being plain Ginny Browne, forget the self-importance of Virginia Martyn-Browne. And that might open an escape route—another comforting idea—if she should take an instant dislike to the man she had come to see. She could think up some excuse and leave, and he would be none the wiser.

But it was useless—she found herself gazing at her own reflection in polished copper walls which were a little distorted but all the more realistic for that. What she saw was far from reassuring: all her assumed insouciance began to evaporate.

Deep-set dark eyes, which she had been told could seduce and entrance, were now wide with shock and terror, and she could no longer understand or even begin to recall the primitive urge which had brought her here in search of her elusive background. As if it had any importance—it wasn't that she had been deprived...

Lips pale, she saw the tip of her tongue slip over them, her face colourless, drab. She very much doubted that Mr Hugo Vanbrugh would be impressed by her appearance. Only the dark hair, belling above ashen features, hidden gleams hinting, wrongly, at hours spent in front of a cheval glass with a silver brush, gave any distinction.

'Mr Hugo's offices.' She had missed the soft warning ping of the lift but the attendant's voice drew her attention to the now open doors and, further, to the spacious landing, deep carpeting and bowls of flowers. 'His secretary's door is at the far side. Thank you and have a nice day.'

And that, decided Ginny as she advanced into the silent world of antique side-tables, elegantly shaded lamps and discreet paintings, was very much a forlorn hope, but... It would be madness to chicken out, having come so far, having spent so many lonely, distressed hours tossing and turning, trying to reach a decision. She strode forward, fastened a confident smile on her face and opened the door that the attendant had indicated.

'May I help you?' Everything about the woman—clipped voice, perfectly smooth blonde hair brushed back from regular features—was straight out of

Hollywood. Even the wonderfully plain navy suit with its short jacket and sparkling white blouse was perfect for her role. Ginny had the feeling that when she stood her legs would be long, like those of a ballerina.

'I would like to see Mr Hugo Vanbrugh, please.' This woman could intimidate with a raised eyebrow, reducing Ginny from high-flying lawyer to office junior.

'Do you have an appointment?' Since she knew the answer to that, the query was mere rhetoric.

'No, I don't.' Ginny gave a smile, deceptively calm and wholly at odds with the tempestuous beating of her heart. 'But he'll see me if you would be kind enough to give him my name.'

'I'm afraid that is impossible.' The woman—Karen Lavery, according to the sign on her desk—shook her head. 'Mr Vanbrugh is operating on a tight schedule.' She had the maddening habit of switching on a dazzling smile, then as you began to respond it disappeared. 'In fact, it is company policy. He never agrees to see anyone without a prior appointment, otherwise there would be chaos.' The on/off smile was nothing less than an accusation.

'Except, of course—' Ginny refused to allow herself to be intimidated—or at least to show she was '—the rules are being broken all the time.'

'Not with—' Karen broke in, but she was meeting Ginny at her most determined.

'And if you tell him that Ginny Browne, of Brockway and Laffan in the City of London—' she handed over the heavily embossed card which detailed an impressive list of qualifications '—on a matter of considerable importance and confidentiality, I'm sure you will find him willing to make an exception.'

'Well…' The blonde's smile grew noticeably more strained, and she scribbled on a sheet of paper ripped from a pad and rose from behind her desk. She was not as tall as Ginny had supposed—legs shorter. The observation was mean but pleasing. 'Please wait here.'

Resentment barely disguised, she went to a concealed door, closed it carefully behind her and reappeared a moment later. 'Very well.' Her voice was still more clipped and disapproving. 'Mr Vanbrugh can spare you just four minutes. Please don't delay him; he has an impossible timetable.'

On legs which had turned to jelly Ginny entered the huge office. Wraparound windows offered a view of the fabulous backdrop of New York City, to which she was at first oblivious as she looked round the apparently empty room. Then she heard a soft chuckle behind the wide desk and the back of a revolving chair swung slightly, the top of a dark head appeared, and her heart gave a fevered leap.

'Yeah…' Another amused growl, an impression of a…of a younger man than…

Then the conversation was ended, the receiver was replaced and the chair swung round to face her.

The figure uncurled itself from the black leather chair—he was tall enough to have played basketball with the Harlem Globetrotters. But how frustrating that she was unable to see his face, with the light behind him and with her looking directly into the glare…

'Miss…' A brief consultation of his note. 'Miss Ginny Browne?' The voice was deep and mellow, one that started all kinds of reaction in the pit of her stomach. 'Of Brockway and Laffan. And what is your business with Vanbrugh Associates, Miss Browne?' While speaking he came round from the expanse of mahogany and perched on one corner, a highly polished shoe swinging gently.

He was a tall man, powerfully built without being the least overweight. His jacket had been left slung over the back of his chair but the trousers were dark and formal, with a tiny red stripe, and accompanied by a white shirt, and a tie in restrained whorls of navy and red. She was still having trouble focusing and…

'Not with Vanbrugh Associates.' It was becoming more of an effort to keep up the pretence of calm self-assurance; all the carefully rehearsed explanations had evaporated, driven out by the realisation that something was terribly wrong. If only she could see his face clearly she might be able to… 'But with you personally. That is… You are Mr Hugo Vanbrugh, aren't you?'

'Yes, I am.' He was relaxed. She caught the glint of white teeth and had an impression of close appraisal, feeling that no detail of her appearance was escaping his notice. Then he twisted slightly so that, for the first time, light slanted across his face and she was offered a glimpse of his eyes—densely blue, almost violet, and certainly the most beautiful she had ever seen in such an unambiguously masculine face.

A powerful man in every sense of the word. And exciting—that was something about which she must remain detached. For a split second she wondered why that was so essential…

'What is your business with me, Miss Browne?'

And in that instant she found the answer—how could she miss it, when it was staring her in the face? But that did not mean it was easy for her to accept it. In fact her startled cry was a denial. She felt the ground begin to undulate beneath her feet. The dark blue carpet was rising to meet her, and… This was all wrong; there was no way this man was the one she had come so far to trace.

For one thing, deep in her brain was a powerful rejection of that possibility—a rejection which brought with it a curious sense of relief. And, for another, he was the wrong generation. This man, this Hugo Vanbrugh, could be no more than thirty-five. Much too young to be the father she had never seen, whose existence she had not suspected until recently, in search of whom she had made this precipitate trip to the States. Reality began to slip away from her, then; she felt herself being drawn into a yawning black abyss and welcomed it.

'Take it easy.' Emerging from the bottomless pit, Ginny found she was lying on a leather settee. A damp towel was being applied to her head, and a voice was expressing sympathy.

'I'm so sorry.' Raising weighted eyelids, she found her brain at once distracted by a problem—that a man should have such amazing eyes, such an unusually dark violet, and when showing deep concern as they were now… Her blouse was threatening to part from her waistband; she struggled to sit up in a more composed way.

'I can't imagine how that happened.' Sheer nervous tension and excitement, most likely—fatigue from the flight, lack of food, all could have contributed. The secretary was there in attendance, too, much more cynical and suspicious than her employer. Ginny felt a blush starting, pulled again at her blouse and swung her feet determinedly onto the floor.

'Don't rush it...'

'I've never fainted before.' She tried to summon a smile but it was wobbly and insecure. 'I ought to have given myself time to recover from the flight before rushing...'

'Ah...you've just arrived. Then that explains it.' He had this curious air, tense but relaxed. 'Maybe some tea, Karen?' He raised an eyebrow in the direction of his secretary. 'You wouldn't mind fixing that for us, would you?'

'Of course not.' The cool glance was for Ginny, the smile for the man. 'Which would you prefer, Miss Browne? Tea or coffee?'

'Right now, I can't imagine anything nicer than a cup of tea. If it's no trouble.'

When they were alone together Ginny smiled ruefully, brown eyes gleaming with a touch of self-mockery. 'I'm afraid I'm taking up your time for no reason. You see, when I asked to see Mr Hugo Vanbrugh I was expecting a much older man. I think...' This was the crux of the whole issue. Her entire future seemed to depend on his answer. 'It must be your father I was hoping to meet—that is, if...'

How to ask delicately if his father was still alive? Or if the other should be his uncle, his cousin, even… Waiting for his reply, she found she was holding her breath.

'My father, Miss Browne, is, I assure you, fit and well and still running this company very efficiently.'

'Oh.' His father! For no immediately obvious reason his assurance caused a tiny ache in the region of her heart but the arrival of the tea-tray was a distraction, a diversion from the need to analyse and dissect. Numbly she watched as the things were placed on a low table close to the settee.

'Thank you.' He gave a swift upward glance at the secretary, who paused with her hand on the doorknob.

'You will remember, Jake, you have an appointment with the chairman of Genesis Holdings.'

'Ah…' He glanced at his watch.

From her position to his left Ginny could see that the wafer-thin gold disc, gold mesh bracelet and cufflinks, also in gold, were disappearing as he shrugged his arms into the jacket rescued from the back of his chair. A slender dark finger checked his shirt collar; he stretched his neck briefly and adjusted his tie.

'That gives us—what? About two minutes would you say, Karen?' He dismissed the woman, who was so clearly disapproving, with a smile. 'Well, maybe you can stall him for a bit. You'll try anyway, won't you?'

And he hooked a chair with one foot, sat opposite Ginny and poured tea into two cups, one of which he handed across, offering sugar and milk as well as a plate of tiny sugary biscuits. 'I'm sorry about the rush, Miss Browne.'

'No.' She was aware of being hideously intrusive, knowing only too well what unscheduled visitors could do to a carefully arranged timetable. 'No, I'm the one who must apologise—I've taken an unfair amount of your time already. But, you see…' Her mind raced and the truth seemed to adapt to the peculiar circumstances. 'Your father and…and mine were great friends long ago…in Hong Kong…and since…' She must be careful, remember what she was saying. Even the slightest hint could have disastrous consequences.

'I tell you what.' Draining his cup, he stood up. 'I'm due to speak with my father later this evening. I can let him know you're here, and…'

'Maybe…' She felt a compulsion to equivocate, possibly because her feelings about the whole mission were so confused. She was so much less certain than she had been at first. 'Maybe he won't want to…he might have forgotten…'

'I'm sure that won't be the case, since he and your father were such friends, but, what I was going to suggest was to let me take you to dinner tonight, and then I can let you know.'

'Oh.' Most of her instinct was to seize the offer with both hands—there was just the tiniest sense of caution and reserve. 'I think I have imposed enough already…'

'You haven't imposed. Besides…' His eyes seemed unwilling to leave hers. They were so disturbing in their intense scrutiny. 'I want to see you again.

Nothing—' his sudden grin was brilliant and earth-shaking '—nothing at all to do with any friendship which existed between our parents. I shall collect you at…say…would seven-thirty be all right?'

'Seven-thirty would be perfect,' she said, meaning it. She rose, picked up her bag and turned to the door. 'But, oh…' She put her hand on the doorknob and paused. 'Your secretary called you Jake just now.' She lowered her voice as if there was the chance of Karen hearing their conversation through the heavy door. 'That was what threw me—at first, you see, I did ask for Mr Hugo Vanbrugh.'

'Ah, well, there is just one Hugo Vanbrugh, and, though I was christened with the same name, I've always been known by my second one to avoid confusion.'

'Ah, that explains it, then.'

'I look forward to seeing you later. Which hotel are you staying at?'

'The Excelsior,' she replied.

There was all the time in the world as Ginny made her way back through the bustling, lively streets for her to reconsider and regret so much lying and deceit. How much wiser to have avoided the folly of further contact with the son when her whole concern was with the father, and the very fact of that connection wholly precluded the possibility of more than friendship between her and Jake Vanbrugh. A shudder ran through her. It was a most melancholy thought—possibly the lowest point in the whole wretched business.

When she reached the hotel foyer she was achingly

weary. Having misjudged the distance, she had been walking for more than an hour, so in the bedroom, she leaned her head against the door for a few moments before going to her as yet unpacked suitcase.

After rummaging for a few minutes her fingers came up against a hard square package which she stared at, filled with regret that it hadn't been disposed of years ago. And she wished with a quite desperate longing, for her days of lost innocence, before the shock of her mother's death in that car crash. That had been more than enough for anyone to cope with. And then to find that her entire existence was based on a lie…

It had been such a bitter, ghastly time. Looking back now, it took on the quality of a nightmare—there were days when she was certain it had happened to someone else, when she was sure she would wake and find all was well, that she wasn't involved in this cruel history which was turning her life upside down. But in her hands she held the evidence—undeniable, absolute.

It had been weeks after the accident before she could bring herself to start the task of clearing out the family home, but at length, refusing the offers of help from various friends, she'd steeled herself and had begun to make some headway.

She had been sitting in the small room which her mother had designated the sewing room, the beauty of the spring day with the sun streaming through high arched windows and all the daffodils planted by her parents stirring gently in the breeze adding a poignant touch. Then she'd reached down for the wrapped and taped package at the bottom of the now almost empty blanket chest. And in that instant her life had fallen apart.

Even now she found it difficult to believe that Tom Browne, who had died two years previously, the man who had been such a tender and devoted father to her, was in fact unrelated by blood. Her own existence was due to a brief and very passionate affair her mother had had in Hong Kong.

The whole story was contained in the diary, in the few letters which had been hidden away for so many years and which, for all Ginny knew, would never have been revealed but for the car crash. But for the devastating suddenness of that event her mother would, in all likelihood, have destroyed the package.

Desolated by the loss of both her parents within such a short time, Ginny had found her anguish compounded by the new disclosures. Any doubts she might have clung to had been blown away by the letter her mother had written to Colonel Hugo Vanbrugh, addressed to the Military Division of the American Embassy in Saigon.

It was a passionate letter, but also touching and rather frightened, telling him that as a result of their affair she was pregnant. But the letter had never been posted, possibly because—and this was made much clearer in the diaries—they had already decided to part.

Reading the fevered soul-searching, the intensely private baring of feelings, Ginny had felt intrusive but, because of her own deep involvement, the story had been irresistible. Even various things which had vaguely puzzled her over the years were, in part, explained. Those times when her mother had seemed withdrawn, when it had seemed all her thoughts and emotions were elsewhere. It was easy now to understand.

Just once in a while there had been glimpses of a more passionate woman than the one who had kept her feelings under such strict control, while her father... Ah, well, not really that, it seemed, but the man who would always be regarded as such. Tom Browne had been placid, calm, even-tempered—a good man, a kind husband and father—but not, one might have thought, the kind of man who would have attracted Jane...

Often Ginny had mused on the apparent disparity, but then what child hadn't pondered the improbability of sexual attraction between its parents? But what was true in this case was that Jane Browne had been an extremely striking woman, beautiful even in middle age, while Tom had been simply an average Englishman, neither good-looking nor particularly plain. But perhaps when they were both young—at least Jane had been young when they'd met and married—things might have been different.

It was so difficult to judge these things when the experience of her own generation was so very different. Intelligent women nowadays did not see marriage as any kind of goal—in fact, the very idea of any woman committing herself for life at nineteen was difficult to understand...

Tom had been an army dentist when they'd met in Germany, where Jane's father, also an army man, had been serving, and… Oh…it was impossible to judge these things—a youngish major, a pretty girl; they could even have fallen madly in love.

The one thing that was abundantly clear was that when Jane had been on her own in Hong Kong for a few weeks—Tom back in London on some kind of military course—she had met Hugo Vanbrugh and there had been instant attraction. Neither had been willing or able to control their feelings, that much was obvious in the one letter from him—several thin, yellowing pages folded inside the back cover of the journal, pages in which Hugo bared his soul, and damned fate that they hadn't met before committing themselves to others.

The diaries reflected some of the anguish Jane had suffered in trying to cast aside the religious scruples which forbade divorce—she had so longed to be free of them, but in the end she'd admitted that abandoning them could possibly poison any happiness she and Hugo could have together.

As it is, I know I have betrayed Tom and my marriage, and I shall suffer lifelong remorse, but, Hugo, I shall always give thanks that you were sent to me. And I shall love you for the rest of my life.

The farewell letter she had written to him twenty-seven years ago, after their decision to part, was touching in its intensity, even though it began with the caveat that she did not know if she would ever send it, but it was sealed and stamped—and wept over, if Ginny's interpretation of the blotches was correct.

I'm torn, because I feel it is your right to know I am going to have your child. And yet what good can it do? More anguish for everyone will result— for you and your family, too, perhaps. You know I'm very fond of Tom and don't want to hurt him any more than I have already done, but you know, too, that when we married I had no idea what real love was about. Even afterwards I wondered what all the fuss was for. Then, Hugo, I met you and I knew.

I think I conceived two weeks ago, on that last fraught night we spent together. Such joy and such despair. But Tom returns tomorrow, and if, as we planned, our lives return to normal, then he will never know the child is not his. What possible good would it do to tell him and break his heart? You see, he loves me.

The letter continued for several pages of intimate reminiscences, with a postscript saying that she had decided against further contact and then a last note with Ginny's name and date of birth.

In the months between her discovery and her journey to New York thoughts of her mother and Hugo Vanbrugh had dominated Ginny's mind. Had Jane intended one day that her daughter should find out the truth about her birth? Or had she meant eventually to destroy the evidence? It was something she would never know and, in a way, that very uncertainty had brought her to the United States.

By seven-fifteen Ginny had got herself entirely under control. All the foolish reactions to the man she had met earlier in the day were totally unbalanced—the result of too many emotional upheavals and an over-active imagination. Recent events had left her in a vulnerable state; add to that her sudden black-out and it was little wonder that Jake Vanbrugh had come over as a cross between Sir Galahad and Richard Gere.

In any event she had never been particularly susceptible to handsome men, and now was most definitely not the time to start. She gave her reflection a sardonic grin.

On the other hand it was good to be able to take a certain amount of complacent assurance from her appearance. The calf-length skirt swaying above shiny black boots was smart and sophisticated enough for wherever he planned to take her. The green silky material clung lovingly to her slender figure, picking up all kinds of subtle shades where the light caught it. The white lawn blouse was full-sleeved and billowy, elaborately tucked and with a prim high collar which made her hold her head proudly. She wore earrings, too, antique silver set with brilliants, which glittered against her dark hair.

Generally, she could see the rest had done her good. A sparkle had returned to the luminous brown eyes, a faint blush to the creamy cheeks—and if the whole was enhanced by a skilled hand with make-up, so what? Her pleased smile was entrancing; the new lipstick in a silky shade of plum suited her wide mouth and exaggerated the white teeth.

'How convenient, Tom,' she remembered a friend remarking, 'that your daughter should be such a wonderful advertisement for your craft.'

And all the time…

A familiar ache returned to her chest, but at that very instant the telephone rang. Her escort, she was told, was waiting, and her heart gave a tiny plop. She forced herself to sit calmly for half a minute before picking up her bag, pulling the door behind her and walking to the lift as sedately as if she had an appointment with her bank manager.

But he was as disturbingly good-looking as she had imagined. Her fainting fit, her empty stomach, the stress—all had nothing to do with it. The realisation was seriously unwelcome. Watching him turn when he heard the lift doors, she held her breath, then, with a determined attempt to distract, found herself taking mental notes.

The hair—which she had thought as dark as sable—had, with the glow of a lamp behind his head, a suggestion of chestnut in it, but that disappeared when he came forward, hand extended.

'Ah…' His mouth curved upwards in appreciation, those splendid violet eyes gleaming as they absorbed each detail of her appearance from the sheen of silky hair to the full mouth—his interest in which she found more than a little disturbing.

She could not say what banal greetings were exchanged before, a moment later, they were being driven off in his limousine. The vehicle purred effortlessly, edging its way through heavy traffic, finally pulling into the parking area of a small, unobtrusive restaurant just off the main thoroughfare.

'Thanks, Steve. Give us about two—two and a half hours.'

The uniformed chauffeur helped her from the car and then she was being guided inside. And if the outside was unobtrusive, the inside was subdued luxury. This was instantly obvious.

They soon ordered and were sipping a chilled Catawba which Ginny found deliciously reviving. He leaned forward, elbows resting on the glossy white cloth, perceptive eyes ranging over her features in a way she could only describe as seductive, 'Now tell me, what exactly is it you would like to speak with my father about?'

With meticulous care she put down her glass, eyes lowered protectively as she considered how to deal with any sudden surge of nerviness. Now she was in control, all wide-eyed innocence as she switched her attention abruptly to his face. 'Has he—has he asked you to filter any message to me?'

'No.' A dark eyebrow was raised in surprise—she wondered if her words had roused some momentary suspicion. 'No. Unfortunately I was unable to contact him, but I shall be seeing him at the weekend and… No, the question was on my own account and merely because I am curious.'

'Ah.' A touch of colour warmed her cheeks, brought an added gleam to her eyes. Above all she must seem sincere. 'There isn't a great deal to tell. Among my parents' things…'

'Are they both dead, your parents?'

'Yes, my father died two years ago and my mother…she was in a car crash earlier this year.' It was dismaying to hear her voice shake. She had been convinced that she had passed through the grievously wounded stage. Now she bit fiercely at her lower lip. 'They were both too young. Dad sixty, Mum not quite fifty.'

'That is sad.' There was a pause before he went on. 'And you were left alone?'

'Yes. No brothers or sisters.' The idea of being alone, the one she had been trying to ignore, made her draw in a deep breath. Quickly she tried to force her thoughts along a different path, but he was not going to allow that.

'And you were saying…?' He was gently persuasive. 'Among your parents' things…?'

'Ah, yes.' Her fingers played with the stem of her wineglass. 'Among their things were some letters, one or two mementoes, and a tiny picture with a note attached with detailed plans about how, at some time in the not too distant future, they meant to contact Hugo. They were planning a long tour of the States when Dad retired.'

That, at least, was true, although the reason for it was not what she was implying. She was certain that the two men had never met—certainly nothing she had read suggested that such a meeting had ever taken place.

With a tremendous effort she was able to control her feelings, was able, even, to produce a wan smile and a shrug—which, to her companion, seemed hopeless—vulnerable rather than philosophical. 'It simply goes to show one should do things when one can, not plan for a future which can so easily…elude one.'

'We should all remember that.' He touched her hand sympathetically, removing his almost at once, just as she became aware of a powerful and affecting reaction. Fortunately there was a diversion as plates were placed in front of them, napkins shaken out…

'And this company you work for…' He handed her the pepper mill, watched as she ground the spice over broiled lobster, his mouth curving in amusement as it was handed back. 'This Brockway and Laffan—it does exist, I suppose?'

'Of course.' Her eyes widened in mock reproof. 'How can you doubt it? They are one of the oldest chambers in the City.'

'And your position with them?'

'Is a very junior one. I've been there since I qualified, three years ago, and if I work hard I have hopes of a partnership—a junior partnership—in, oh, in about twenty years' time.'

'As soon as that, eh?' One elbow on the table, a finger moving against the almost smiling mouth, he leaned forward.

The compelling gaze, more violet than blue, held her in an intense, very nearly intimate scrutiny—so intimate that her whole body came alive with the joy of it—pulses throbbing, blood singing, heart pounding, eyes glowing.

'But I shall be surprised, Miss Ginny Browne, to find you still with Brockway and Laffan in two years, let alone twenty.'

'Really?' Silly to sound so breathless, so naïve, when she most certainly was not, when all she was doing was enjoying herself with an intelligent, attractive man and with absolutely no strings. *That* was what made it such a special attraction. 'And where do you imagine I'll be in…yes, let's say in two years' time?'

'Not, I suggest, among the dusty files of one of the oldest firms in the City of London.'

'The oldest firm does not necessarily imply fusty Dickensian premises.'

'Ah, so you're in modern offices?'

'Not exactly.' Later she might explain that they occupied a pair of terraced houses built originally for well-to-do city merchants. Elegant staircases led to the partners' chambers, with masses of highly polished mahogany and brass, and there were walled gardens to the rear, which were fragrant in summer with old-fashioned roses and honeysuckle, pinks and peonies. It was light years from his prestigious penthouse, but there was little doubt as to which she preferred.

'You are being so provoking and evasive, Miss Browne.' He frowned, emphasising the degree of his disapproval by covering her hand with his. The thumb stroked her gently and, though it was difficult to admit, excitingly. His expression continued to show amusement. 'Do they teach that at law school these days?'

'They teach us to be accurate and questioning!' Her manner was tart, a little defensive, and all because of that disturbing touch. If she could extract her hand casually, or… A tiny shudder was repressed. What if she were to obey her instincts, if she were to turn her hand over so their palms were in contact, with the possibility of fingers lacing? Her eyes grew dreamy with longing and there was a powerful but unfamiliar sensation in the pit of her stomach…

And then he moved, severing the moment, the indulgence. She sighed relief and…and she would *not* think of frustration. Hurriedly she tried to backtrack. 'You still haven't answered my question.'

'And that was?'

Now she must keep the conversation light, with no opportunity for emotional complications. 'Where *do* you imagine I shall be in two years' time?' Oh, heavens! Was she being deliberately provocative? Inviting speculation which she hoped would flatter or at least please her?

'Married, I should say was the most likely scenario.'

'Married?' Her tone suggested he'd mentioned a synonym with slavery and bondage. 'But even if I were to marry…' she continued with the pretence that such a circumstance had never entered her mind, longing to grin at herself but managing to keep a straight face. '…and that would be if the worst should happen—that does not mean I would leave the company.'

'It might.' He pursed his lips, his amused expression lingering. 'But, then again, it might not. I concede to that extent.'

The best defence was attack, and at that moment she felt much in need of defence—from her own feelings if from nothing else. 'Now, Mr Vanbrugh, first of all, you don't even know me. I might be already married.'

'No ring.' He caught her left hand, smiling in triumph, and took it to his mouth.

Without an impressive degree of self-control she would surely have flinched, but she was confident her inner turmoil was totally concealed—other than, perhaps, a tiny tremble in her voice which might have given him a clue.

'Neither,' she began firmly, 'do you wear a ring.' They ought not to be going down this road, ought not to be acting in this silly, almost—oh, heavens—almost flirtatious way. At least, *she* ought not to be—he might be excused. 'But I certainly do not make the deduction that you are unmarried...'

'It would be the right one.'

His reply in itself might have set off alarm bells, but all she was aware of was a throb of satisfaction. 'Nevertheless, it need not have been.'

'Are you telling me...?' When she pulled gently, he released her hand. 'Are you telling me I was wrong to draw implications from the absence of a ring?'

'Not exactly,' she said primly, repressing the desire to smile but capitulating when he grinned.

'I rest my case.' Both of them sat back, smiling at each other, while waiters came to remove plates and to serve the next course.

It was impossible, she conceded with a tiny pain immediately below her ribs, to pretend she didn't find him dangerously attractive. In a room full of good-looking, wealthy men he stood out. That was not simply her own opinion—more than one woman in their immediate neighbourhood would probably be willing to neglect her escort for Jake Vanbrugh. That he had been recognised when they arrived was obvious—he had exchanged casual greetings with several couples but had shown no signs of wishing to linger or introduce them to Ginny.

They were drinking strong black coffee when he dropped his bombshell, one which made her crash down her cup and look at him in consternation. 'On Saturday, Ginny, I'm going down to Richmond to visit my parents. I want you to come with me.'

'What?' She frowned, taking a moment to allow her brain to absorb the implications. Then her reaction was immediate. 'Oh, no. I couldn't possibly; I wouldn't dream of intruding.' The whole situation was getting out of hand. It was Mr Hugo Vanbrugh she had come all this way to see; there had been no intention of becoming involved with other members of his family.

She felt a sob begin to rise in her throat as thoughts of her own deceit began to hit her. She had meant to be so *honest*, so understanding. Certainly the last thing in her mind had been the possibility of some kind of perverse emotional entanglement. But she could at least nip that in the bud—she herself was the only one who might suffer and...

'You wouldn't be.' The flimsy excuse was disregarded the instant it was uttered, and with the smiling charm which was proving impossible to resist.

They decided to stroll back to her hotel. The limousine was dismissed and it was impossible for Ginny to deny the pleasure of the experience—being with a handsome man with unobtrusive good manners, added to a certain amount of euphoria engendered by the wine…

'My parents are hospitable people,' he continued, his hand touching her elbow to warn of an obstruction in their path. 'And I know they would love to see you.'

Now his touch became more of a threat. He seemed to be tempting her into a trap of her own making, arousing feelings she was reluctant to face, and her shiver was an involuntary reaction.

'You're cold. I knew we should have been driven.'

'No, I'm not cold.' She took a firm grip of herself. 'Not in the very least. It was simply… Anyway…' A change of subject was indicated, before she lost herself in a maze of unconvincing explanations. 'I don't feel I can go, Jake, I… I took only a few days off work…'

'You won't see my father otherwise. He and my mother are off on a cruise next week, so…you'd best fly down with me if you want to see him.'

They had reached the hotel and went in and sat down in the foyer, deserted now but for the young man who sat yawning behind the reception desk.

'Besides, apart from that—' his eyes were signalling a message she hardly dared translate '—*I* want to see you again.'

His swift, unexpected touch, just the brush of a finger against her cheek, brought her heart leaping in wild agitation.

'More than that, I'm determined on it. You may not know it—' he leaned forward, his manner becoming more intimate '—but Hugo Vanbrugh is a very determined man, used to getting his own way, and I'm cast in the same mould as my father.' He smiled as if his words were not to be taken entirely literally— he might even have been amused by her wide-eyed expression of shock.

Yes, she thought numbly, she *could* see that Hugo Vanbrugh was someone very used to having his own way—she was living proof of that, and she felt a stab of disgust. What kind of man was it who would seduce a lonely young wife? It was convenient to forget her mother's willing participation... Then Jake's voice brought her back from her reverie.

'But you look tired. Why don't you go up to bed now?' Automatically she allowed herself to be led to the lift, and stood waiting while it was summoned. 'Have a good night's sleep.' Again a finger brushed tenderly, this time against her mouth. 'I shall have Karen bring over all the details tomorrow and I shall pick you up here on Saturday morning. Goodnight.'

Leaning back in the furthest corner of the lift, she watched the doors slide closed to exclude him. Only then did she release a great sigh, as if, by some feat of courage and daring, she had escaped encroaching danger. And it was a few seconds before her disordered thoughts were sorted to the extent that she could recognise the exact nature of that danger.

There was only one thing for it: she must leave

New York at the first opportunity—tomorrow morning if possible. There were many places in the States where she could happily spend the rest of her short stay. Boston or St Louis, even Sioux City—anywhere that the Vanbrugh empire was unlikely to extend, and where, perhaps more to the point, Jake Vanbrugh was unlikely to think of looking for her.

Certainly the present situation was one she could never have envisaged. It had all been so carefully plotted—to come and to make the most discreet contact with the man who had fathered her so many years ago. It was not difficult to visualise how much of a shock such a piece of news might be to a happily married man.

She knew few men would welcome such news, and that was why she had been so cautious, why she had concocted such a misleading explanation. She had meant to cause no anxiety—her first concern would have been to assure him there was no threat of exposure. And then after passing on the few things which might have held some sentimental interest for him, they would have said goodbye, she would have returned to her job in London and any future meetings would have been arranged by mutual consent.

It had been her hope, but no more, that their meeting would settle the deep uncertainty which had troubled her after discovering the truth about her birth. And if it didn't then she was determined it would be *her* problem, one she would keep to herself and not expect him to share.

True, there had been the fanciful notion that he

might from time to time visit her in the UK, that they could get to know each other, might even find they liked each other. After all, since her mother had fallen so hopelessly in love with him, and he with her mother, Ginny and he were bound to find some common ground. And, in a strange way, she felt she would be doing something for her mother—completing a story which had been unresolved for more than a quarter of a century.

She reached her bedroom and began, listlessly, to unbutton her blouse. Only, the plans she had made had begun to unravel the moment she'd reached New York. For one thing, on finding the company had offices in the city centre, she had rushed off immediately. Experience ought to have told her it was unlikely she would be ushered into the presence of the top man—life in the higher echelons simply did not work like that and, in any case, what she had most certainly not anticipated was meeting not the man himself, but his son. Still less had her wildest flights of fancy expected that, after a few hours' acquaintance, she would find herself in the gravest danger of falling in love.

There! She had faced up to the dread which had been hovering at the back of her mind all evening. Her knees gave way and she sank onto the bed. Fingers pressed against her mouth, she stared at her reflection in the dressing-table mirror, hardly noticing that her face was drained of colour or that her eyes were wide with shock.

In spite of herself she was reliving that moment in

the restaurant when she'd had that yearning to turn her palm up to his, to feel the brush of sensitive skin on… A shudder of something very close to fear ran through her.

With determination she got up and began to walk about the room, putting clothes away as she made up her mind to deal with the dangers.

If she was to keep on reminding herself that Jake Vanbrugh was her half-brother then all these juvenile feelings would die down. It was most likely all down to the intense emotions of the past months, plus the very fact of arriving in New York. The combination was more than enough to knock anyone off balance.

Slightly more relaxed, she pulled her nightdress over her head and went into the bathroom to brush her teeth. Tomorrow she would leave a polite little note for Jake, letting him know that a distant cousin had flown in from Nova Scotia and had persuaded her to join a trip to Niagara Falls. The permutations were endless.

Ginny pulled the light-cord and stood in the half-dark, dreading that moment when the bedside lamp would be extinguished and she would face the bleak terror of the night. There was a word used to describe illicit feelings between certain blood relatives, one from which she shrank with disgust.

But it was firmly lodged there at the back of her mind and she could drive it out only by seeing Jake Vanbrugh as he was—her half-brother. She had to find the strength to take him up on his invitation, to fly down to Richmond with him. It was the only way she would be forced to face the truth and to see Jake Vanbrugh as *her* father's son. That was what he was and always would be. Nothing less, and certainly nothing more.

CHAPTER TWO

GINNY moved among the guests, smiling, exchanging pleasantries, answering the various queries about herself. It was the kind of life to which it would be dangerously easy to become addicted. Alone for a moment, determined to ignore the strange feeling of discomfort in her chest, she stood back, taking in the sheer elegance of the room.

Three high arched windows were thrown open to the covered terrace, where friends lingered chatting. Beyond that were acres of immaculate lawn. There were rose bushes, each blooming, or so it seemed, at the height of its fragrant perfection. And so many beautifully dressed people, iced drinks clinking, all so animated, friendly and sophisticated.

It was everything that came to mind when one considered these East Coast states. Richmond was very nearly a caricature of itself—the very scene one would have lapped up in a glitzy TV miniseries.

Inside, too, there was so much good taste in the discreet furnishings, which ranged through soft creams to the more subtle gamboge and tawny golds. Pale walls were the perfect backdrop for the small collection of modern paintings, while at the far end the grand piano—music by Chopin on the stand—was waiting for the hostess to sit and entertain her guests.

'Ginny, my dear.' The slow, drawling tones of that

very woman made Ginny turn and fix a smile firmly on her mouth. 'I hope my son isn't neglecting you. I do so want everyone to enjoy the afternoon.'

'No.' How breathless and unsure she sounded. Not at all like Mrs Vanbrugh. 'I'm enjoying myself enormously. It's a real pleasure to spend time in such lovely surroundings, meeting such friendly people. And I have a drink here.' She reached for the glass of mint julep and sipped appreciatively. 'Mmm. Delicious. And once again, my very best wishes for your anniversary. A ruby wedding is something rather special.'

'Thank you, my dear. We have been very lucky, Hugo and I. Oh...' She glanced over Ginny's shoulder towards the doors which opened into the hall. 'I see him now...and with Jake—isn't that lucky? I did wonder where they had disappeared to. Just wait while I bring them over to you. Don't move now.'

While her hostess walked purposefully towards the doorway Ginny turned and stood, watching, admiring almost everything about the woman she had just met, who had barely blinked at having an uninvited guest thrust on her at such a busy time.

She was small, and her white hair was cut short and waved in a casual flattering style. The striking eyes seemed all she had in common with her son and their colour was enhanced by the violet dress. She was slender and vivacious too, now smiling up at her husband, one hand slipped through his arm and one through that of her son.

Ginny had a strange feeling—as if she were a detached observer. She withdrew a little into the shelter of one of the pillars which held up the canopied roof. Perhaps she wasn't really here at all. Maybe she had stuck to her original intention of bailing out and severing all links with the Vanbrugh family. She wished!

She was watching Hugo Vanbrugh now through slightly narrowed, cynical eyes—he was the very picture of a doting, constant husband, and yet... She forced herself to be less judgemental. It was easy enough to understand past events, to see how her mother had been swept off her feet.

He was tall, but not as tall as his son. Damn. Damn. Damn. Why did she have to make comparisons when she was trying to wipe Jake from her mind? But Hugo was impressive, a man of obvious authority with the glamour of having been a fighting man, which her father, in the medical services, had so clearly lacked.

He was slightly rugged, wearing a light cream-coloured suit of the kind which was almost a uniform in the present company. She watched him link fingers with his wife's, smile lovingly, exude fidelity, and she found she could look no more. Tears stung as she turned away.

Such a scene of marital harmony and felicity... Her early instinct has been right—she should never have come to Virginia with Jake. It was sheer madness to have taken such a risk.

Apart from anything else there had been something strange about her meeting with Hugo, brief though the introduction had been. Something odd and perceptive about the way his eyes had probed, his head held slightly to one side as if picking up vibes, his hand holding hers for a split second longer than had been necessary. She had felt her knees begin to shake and had been grateful for the arrival of a group of guests, with their noise and laughter.

'Miss Ginny.' At that moment of introspection she felt her arm being grasped and, startled, she looked up into the face of someone she had met earlier, a Colonel—an old army colleague of Hugo Vanbrugh.

He was a tall, handsome man, something of a dandy, with his grey moustache parted neatly in the middle and curled to each side into pomaded whiskers on each mahogany-coloured cheek. He was wearing pale striped trousers with his cream jacket, and a blue silk shirt chosen, Ginny was sure, to enhance the blue-grey eyes which sparkled with mischief and the joy of living. A red rose was in his buttonhole, marking the occasion of a ruby wedding.

Without effort, Ginny succumbed to the charming old-world manners, allowing herself to be guided towards one of the open windows, glad of an excuse to escape her pressing concerns for even a short time.

'I've been longing to speak with you, Miss Ginny. I'm so determined, you see, to find out, despite your delightful English accent, if there is any chance that your full name is Virginia and, if so, were you named for our State? I would so love you to confirm both of these facts.'

His words made another small piece of the jigsaw drop into position. She felt a momentary shock, though she was confident nothing in her manner had betrayed her, her voice remaining calm and unruffled as she would have wished. 'You're right about my name being Virginia, though no one has ever used the full name.' She affected sadness, apologised prettily with hands outstretched in a gesture of regret. 'But I'm afraid I know of no connection with the State. My parents, as far as I know, chose the name simply because they liked it.' Lies came so easily to the tongue when they were so assiduously practised.

'Well, I'm real sorry about that.' His cheerful expression was a comfort. 'I was about to ask Hugo…' His eyes narrowed, became more searching. 'You remind me… I don't suppose you and I have met before, have we?'

Ginny's heart gave a great leap. She breathed in slowly, then quite deliberately she raised her glass and sipped from it before replacing it on a table. 'Colonel…' There was a gurgle of humour in her voice, and she shook her head with another regretful smile, 'I should certainly have remembered if we had. You are not the kind of man I should have been likely to forget.'

A practised flatterer himself, he was able to smile when he saw the tables turned. 'How very disappointing.' The appreciative eyes sparkled down at her.

'Colonel.' The deep voice from behind made Ginny turn as Jake put a possessive hand on her elbow. 'Why is it you always monopolise the prettiest girl in the room?'

'I suppose—' the older man shrugged modestly '—you could put it down to practice.'

'More than likely.' Jake grinned. 'I've been looking everywhere for Ginny, then I caught sight of you out here and I knew where she would be. Do you mind if I steal her away for a few moments?'

'I mind, darn it. Of course I mind. But I can quite see she might prefer your company to mine.'

'You mustn't say such things, Colonel, I've loved talking with you.' It was more a desperate gesture towards common sense than the strict truth.

'Thank you, my dear, you are very kind—but an old campaigner knows when the time has come to make a tactical retreat. I fear I stand little chance with Jake around—though if I had been twenty, or even ten years younger, I might have given him a run for his money. But off you go.' He was being mockingly flirtatious. Raising Ginny's hand, he took it to his lips, and she felt the brush of silky hair against her skin. 'I hope to see you before you leave for England, Miss Virginia. And in the meantime...' He frowned, searching her features closely. 'I shall try to remember.'

As they crossed the lawns Ginny felt her agitation mount. Suppose he did remember...suppose he had at some time met her mother, and began to jump to conclusions. Suppose...

'The Colonel,' Jake said softly into her ear, 'is the local "Don Juan"—a great ladies' man.'

'I think I guessed as much.' She was surprised her voice sounded so calm, so unruffled, but the opportunity was too good to miss. 'But he is a bit older than your father?'

'Mmm. Considerably.'

'So...did he serve in Vietnam as well?'

'Oh, no. He had retired long before that. But you must ask Dad if you want to know more about that.'

'Ah.' So he could not have known her mother. She hurried on. 'And is there a Mrs Colonel?'

'No. He has been chased from one end of the county to the other but no one has been skilful enough to catch him. Come on—' seizing her hand, he hurried her towards a clump of trees '—I want to show you the lake.'

And, in spite of everything, in spite of knowing all the risks, as she did, she allowed herself to be guided along a path through the wooded area well away from the house, and there, wandering among the trees in the dappled heat of the perfect afternoon, she lost all the will to resist.

She would *not* close her mind to the dangers—that was a promise fervently made—but what was wrong with enjoying the touch of his fingers on her inner wrist for a few brief minutes? It was such bliss, and there was no harm when...

'Ginny.' They had reached the edge of the small lake, and stood together for a moment watching flies dance on the golden haze above the surface. Occasionally there was a widening ring on the water, streaked pink and gilt by the late sunshine, while at the far side, among clumps of sedge, a family of water fowl floated, preened and dived. It might have been the Forest of Arden, certainly it had that same air of enchantment, and for a moment it seemed possible to enter that magic world, to find solutions to what was insoluble.

And Jake was turning her towards him, his index finger lightly tracing the line of her jaw. 'Virginia.' The name lingered on his tongue, mingling with a groan, as if even its familiarity had taken on a whole new meaning. 'I can hardly believe we've known each other for just two days and yet…and yet…' Intense blue eyes burned down into hers, his voice deepened. 'I feel I've always known you. At least, I've suspected, *hoped* you were out there somewhere, waiting for me to find you.'

His words were such an echo of her own feelings that she knew a moment's sheer exultation, so intense and powerful as to frighten her after a moment into sense and even banality. 'Yes.' Her tone was considering, slightly doubtful, and her jaw was rigid with the strain of her false smile. 'Well, what I find so marvellous is that everyone is so friendly. Your mother didn't even blink when we arrived today, right in the midst of the preparations for the party.'

'Well, Mother takes everything in her stride. She is the world's best organiser.'

Not unlike her own mother. The bleak thought was like another reminder. 'You realise, of course, that if I had known about their anniversary before you popped it out at me on the plane nothing would have persuaded me to come?' Hard to imagine a less appropriate visitor at their family celebration, on the lines of the wicked fairy at the christening, though maledictions were not in her plan.

'Nonsense.' He dismissed her protestations with easy confidence. 'They are all thrilled to have you, though I confess they're going to be taken aback to discover you're not exactly what you appear to be.'

'What?' His words caused a throb of anxiety bordering on real fear. She was becoming so enmeshed in deceit she would soon be unable to pick her way through all the lies. 'What on earth do you mean?'

'Well, I suspect—' he grinned '—in fact I'm sure they've got the idea that you and I are... Well, I'm not in the habit of flying down from New York with girls in tow.'

'Oh, I'm sorry. I hope it won't make things difficult for you when they find out the truth. I mean...' She felt colour rise in her cheeks. 'I mean when your father knows it's really him I came to see.' She hoped her detached tone might cool the situation just a little, and certainly when he answered he was a little more thoughtful.

'Funnily enough I don't think he has the faintest idea. Certainly he showed no sign when he heard your name, though Browne, even with an e, is fairly common.'

'Oh.' Now was the moment to begin to clear up at least a minor deceit. 'Maybe I can explain that. He would know my...my parents as Martyn-Browne, but when Dad left the army he dropped the first part. He thought it was pretentious and had been tacked on just a generation or so ago. A bit of a relief, really—some of these double-barrelled names can be quite a mouthful.' Her smile was tentative, apologetic, even. 'Can you imagine, ''Virginia Martyn-Browne''?'

'Ah.' He looked steadily down at her for what seemed a long time. 'And what other secrets have you been hiding from me, Miss Martyn-Browne?'

For a moment her heart seemed to stand still, then it was racing hectically. But, with an effort, she forced herself to answer lightly. 'So many I don't know where to begin.' It was a relief to see him smile, and she felt she could hurry on. 'But perhaps it was a mistake—first of all coming down here, but, more than that, hiding the real reason for my visit. On reflection, it might have been better to explain at once.'

'Mmm.' Jake considered. 'But that will be resolved this evening, when all the guests have gone and we're having a family dinner, just the four of us.'

She spoke slowly, sorrowfully, voicing thoughts which had been on her conscience since the early moments of their acquaintance. 'You know, you are very trusting, Jake. You have only my word that I'm who I say I am, that your father and mine were so very friendly all those years ago. I could be perpetrating the most enormous con trick.'

And I am, she admitted silently. How often in the courts I have seen and heard the lies with which people use and abuse each other, and I feel nothing but disgust. Yet here I am, pursuing a most devious line against the kindest people... Tears began to prick at her eyes.

'Are you?' His voice was mellow and amused, a dark slender eyebrow raised in gentle disbelief...

Yes. She wanted to say it, but couldn't. For the simple reason that the truth was not something she could share with Hugo's son. If *he* chose to do so that was a different matter, but it was not her secret. So she managed a false smile. 'I'm not.' Stricken with guilt at her deception, she took refuge in some trite advice. 'But people these days ought not to be so trusting. I might have some dire reason for wishing to infiltrate your family...'

'I'll lock my door tonight as a precaution.' Now his look was teasing but with a hint of a challenge.

'I promise you are quite, quite safe.' Her tone was slightly sharp and the eyes raised to his were brilliant with indignation. As well as frustration.

'You disappoint me.' She found herself manoeuvred against the bole of one of the ancient oaks, and as he spoke in that low disturbing voice he placed one hand flat against the trunk and hooked the other against her waist, pulling her into the curve of his body, effectively overpowering her.

'Jake.' It was a gasp of fear and longing. 'Jake, don't.'

And gently, gently, all his attention on her mouth, he lowered his mouth to hers. She willed him to stop, of course she did, and with a quite desperate longing to be free. She saw him, felt him come nearer, felt his breath on her skin, was close enough to confirm the ridiculous length of the lashes which framed his eyes. And she was losing control, could feel it slipping away from her, and was helpless to do anything about it. Her heart was hammering against her ribs, her legs had turned to water—only the strength of his arm stopped her from slipping to the ground.

It didn't seem possible that what she was engaged in was forbidden, against the laws of nature. Her lips parted to ease her frantic breathing, adding an air of eager collusion.

But his mouth on hers was unbearably sweet, coaxing and tender one moment, irresistibly fierce and demanding a moment later. Very much as Ginny had, in the past forty-eight hours, imagined it would be.

And for the time being all her fears and reservations were submerged in this wash of delicious, sensual indulgence, this opening up, this giving and taking of such mind-blowing pleasure and...

Way at the back of her mind a warning bell sounded. She tried to detach herself—it was wrong, she knew it was and she mustn't carry on. *That* was what she had decided and she would not, *dare* not— even though to resist was torture...

With some firmness and a little protest Ginny put her hands on Jake's chest, pushing him away, hiding her pain as she extricated herself when he would have detained her. 'Don't, Jake.' The words almost stuck in her throat. 'Don't crowd me.' One contrite glance over her shoulder and she began to move with determination in the direction of the house.

'I can't promise that.' He spoke tersely as he began to walk with her, making no attempt to touch, hands thrust into the pockets of his trousers, and frowning.

It seemed necessary to lighten things. 'Well, then, maybe I'm the one who ought to lock my door tonight.'

The moment the words were uttered she wished them unsaid. How could she be so crass as to resurrect that touchy subject? How could she, an experienced lawyer, trained to be clear-headed and single-minded, be so provocative? But even as she asked the question she knew the answer. On the one hand she was rejecting him, on the other it was impossible for her to deny her intense attraction, to pretend this illicit hunger did not exist...

'Maybe you should at that...' Now there was a distinct note of edgy frustration. 'Except—' And he broke off.

'Except?' she prompted, curious.

'Except as a rule I agree with you.' His good humour was at least partly restored. 'I rather agree these things are best taken at a leisurely pace—enjoyed, savoured without being rushed.' They were emerging from the wood and onto the lawn which surrounded the house. He turned, and took her by the shoulders, 'For, you see, I feel we have time, you and I, to get to know each other.'

'Jake.' Surely he would recognise the sound of naked fear in her voice, see it in the emotion-drenched eyes which looked up with such appeal? How could she warn him without being explicit, without wrecking his family? How could she warn herself, for heaven's sake? Help me, Jake! Help me, please!

'What is it, Ginny?' Yes, thank God, his senses were tuned to hers: He'd latched on at once, eyes narrowing as they searched her face. 'Are you trying to tell me you're in a relationship with someone else?'

'Jake...' Her eyes were stinging as she turned away. 'Just don't make a big thing.' Feverishly she tried to deal with her jumbled thoughts and feelings. 'You know I'm twenty-six years old—it would be strange if I hadn't been...wasn't...'

'Are you?' His manner was uncompromising. 'All you have to do is say yes or no.'

'Not *exactly*, but—'

'Not exactly? What the devil does that mean? It's the sort of answer any half-decent attorney would happily trash.'

'Jake.' She was determined to be light-hearted, impossible to provoke. That might be the best diversion. 'I'm not in the habit of discussing my personal life with anyone, especially with someone who is…' The look on his face made her tremble, it was an effort to go on. 'Well, who is almost a stranger.'

'But you know, don't you?' Now he was firm, courteous, and she had the ghastly feeling that he was disappointed at the need to explain. 'We never were strangers, you and I, not from that first moment you appeared in my office in New York.'

'Well…' How could anyone deny such a statement? It would have been a contradiction of life itself and yet, to this one man especially, it would be folly to make such an admission. 'Well, of course, Jake, you must know you are a very attractive man.' The remark caused instant displeasure, apparent in the narrowed eyes, the tightened jaw. 'It would be strange if I hadn't found you easy to talk with.'

'Don't patronise me, damn you.'

'What do you want me to say?' With nerves nearly at breaking point, her temper flared before she could control it. 'Don't be corny?' she almost sneered. 'Would you have preferred that? Anyway—' she bit her lip, ashamed of her outburst '—I certainly did not mean to patronise you.'

Now was a time for total detachment, and her profession had taught her something of that. Her manner became consciously friendly yet uninvolved—she had dealt with dozens of clients in the self-same manner.

'Oh, and Jake?' She resumed her stroll towards the house. 'You know I told you what a shock it was to

find out about the ruby wedding? Would it be possible, do you think, to arrange transport to take me
into town? I would like to buy your parents a small
memento before I leave.'

'Their instructions to all their friends were that
presents were unnecessary, but I know how you feel.
So long as you decide to keep it small.' He kicked
moodily at a tussock of grass. 'But you know they'll
be leaving in the morning, so...'

'So soon? I'd forgotten. Then...' It was becoming
increasingly difficult for her to control her agitation
but it was essential to let him know there were some
decisions she would make for herself. She must *not*
weaken—if she allowed him to control her then soon
all her scruples, all her integrity, would be swept
aside.

At least her voice came out firm and composed. 'If
we do go into town perhaps I can do something about
booking a flight back to New York.'

'I had no idea you were in such a hurry to leave.'
Sarcasm now, to add to her trials.

The disapproval which she had deliberately fos-
tered was hard to bear. 'Well, I cannot impose on your
parents. There's no reason why they should have an
unexpected guest thrust upon them to complicate their
holiday plans.'

'No reason, except that I invited you. And, as far
as booking a flight back goes, I brought you down
and I have every intention of taking you back again.'

Her conscience assailed her; she was seeming so
ungracious, 'Well, it's so much more comfortable in

a private plane, where you can sit and chat with the pilot…'

Ignoring her more conciliatory tone, he returned to the earlier point she had made. 'Besides, you are the daughter of a long-lost friend of the family.'

'Wh-what?' Something in the way he spoke set off the alarm bells, made her heart bound in agitation, her mind veering inevitably to the package in the bottom of her suitcase—heavily taped, admittedly, but with the potentially destructive power of Semtex as far as this family was concerned. With an effort she controlled her wildly active imagination. 'What do you mean, Jake?'

'I mean…' His eyes were searching, a tiny frown signalling some kind of curiosity which had been absent a moment earlier. 'Simply that my parents are Virginians—kind, hospitable people who enjoy nothing more than entertaining friends.'

She was ashamed. How could she have come here in such an underhand way, deceiving people who were prepared to trust her? It wasn't what she had planned, so how had things gone so wrong? But they had, and at that moment she had to deal with the situation.

'I know that, Jake.' Her regret was audible. 'I felt it from the first moment.' And from that first moment her misgivings had multiplied. Oh, to be able to walk away and leave all their lives intact. 'But I must get back to London. I planned only a few days' leave, and…'

'I doubt if they will hold you to that.'

'Perhaps not, but…'

'Anyway, I'm still waiting for an answer to that original query. It is important to me, you know.'

'And the question?' Heat flushed her face at such pretence.

He had changed tactics—now he was light and teasing, which was much more difficult to resist. 'The question was, are you married?'

'I thought you had decided that the other night— you know I'm not.' It was a relief to be honest.

'Engaged?'

'No.' Another easy one. 'I'm not.'

'Or…in a regular relationship?'

'Well…' Time now for evasion. 'I suppose that would depend on what you mean by…'

'You know what I'm asking you, Ginny.'

'Yes, I know.'

'And your answer?'

'Not exactly.'

'Well.' He was smiling down at her as if she had confessed undying passion for him. 'This time I shall take that as a negative.' His voice was lazy and tender, so irresistible in its mellow cadences that she lost the will to argue. 'And that's all right.'

He brushed a wisp of hair back from her face and linked his fingers in hers as they turned to mount the steps of the terrace. It was the sort of gentle contact which was totally unthreatening; it was his words which were so striking.

For she knew it was not all right. Far from that, she was convinced her life would never again be described in those comfortable, casual terms.

CHAPTER THREE

DINNER that night, which Ginny had rather dreaded, and expected to be fraught and awkward, turned out, in the event, to be relaxed and light-hearted once she had decided to ignore the sensation of dropping earthwards in a lift and try to forget her reason for being here. In short, to act as she would at any normal dinner party with people she didn't know all that well.

Except for Jake, that was. Sitting opposite him, it was impossible for her to argue with his earlier statement that they might have known each other for ever. So fervent was her agreement that she could hardly contemplate what would happen when all contact was severed and she returned to London. But in the meantime, she exerted herself to be the interested and interesting guest—a role she could fill easily.

Although it was inevitable that the conversation was concerned mainly with the day's celebrations, with little snippets of gossip about the guests, she was able to play her part well, with one or two amusing anecdotes about her work.

For much of the time, her tensions eased, she was content simply to listen and to soak up impressions of a lifestyle which was so very different from her own—where luxury, horses, private planes and exotic travel were everyday experiences.

Not that their wealth was flamboyantly evident—

the room in which they ate was pretty and practical rather than ostentatious. It was built in an octagonal shape, opening onto a terrace with steps leading down to a circular swimming pool. The table where they sat was round, draped with cream damask, a bowl of red roses in the centre, all festively gleaming with silver and crystal. The food, unobtrusively served by a pleasant middle-aged woman, was delicious but simple—a chilled soup, grilled lamb chops, tiny and meltingly tender, eaten with a plain salad, and fruit and cheese to complete the meal.

Less simple was the champagne which they drank, and which might have been in part responsible for the atmosphere of relaxed pleasure. And beneath it all was the certainty that here was a happy, united family, much as her own had been, taking pleasure in each other's company, sharing interests. And, although Jake was inevitably the one who interested Ginny most, she also liked his mother, while his father...

Well, sitting eating was almost the first chance she had had to form opinions, and turning her head to speak, smiling at some remark, provided a perfect opportunity.

Once or twice she'd had a curious feeling, one difficult to identify but disturbingly positive once she became aware of it. A glance which made her hold her breath, a frisson of familiarity at a particular gesture—and something like a trickle of icy water down her spine when she realised she was recognising something of herself through a slightly distorted mirror. Nothing which would be visible to a casual observer, but here and there a flicker of something she recognised. Spooky. Or perhaps mere auto-suggestion.

In spite of this, she still retained a certain reserve, a prejudice about Hugo Vanbrugh, wholly coloured by what she knew of him—and that was unfair. After all, she harboured no such feelings about her mother. If he had cultivated a false image, then Jane had done it just as effectively, and who was Ginny to blame either?

In fact, irresistibly, her eyes settled on the younger man sitting opposite, his eyes crinkling in amusement at some anecdote, white teeth gleaming against dark skin. She was, for the first time, appreciating how potent a force sexual attraction could be...

All at once she saw she was the focus of his attention. His parents continued to toss light-hearted conversation back and forth while Jake raised his glass in what appeared to be a surreptitious salute. He raised it and sipped, his eyes holding hers over the crystal rim.

Heart beating in quite unreasonable excitement, she felt compelled to return the gesture, her whole body suffused with tension and longings which the wine did little to still.

Then their reverie was interrupted. She saw Jake's eyes move with obvious reluctance towards his father, and an instant later, realised that everyone was waiting for a reply from her.

'I'm sorry.' She coloured guiltily and dabbed with her napkin at her hand, where she had spilled a drop of wine. 'I was still thinking of that story about Jake and the baseball and I didn't quite catch...'

Not for the first time she diagnosed a ruthless streak, a hardness in Hugo Vanbrugh which seemed not to have surfaced in his son…

'I was asking how it happened you and Jake met up, since I gather you have just arrived in the country. I would have thought you'd hardly had the time…' It was the most brutal return to earth, one she wished she might have postponed indefinitely, but…

'Oh. Yes…' If all colour had drained from her face, as she thought probable, none of the others noticed. No one rushed forward to support her so it was reasonable to assume there were no outward signals, for which she ought to be grateful. Inwardly in turmoil, she was clinging desperately to calm, to reason, thrusting aside her inclination to rush screaming from the room.

'I've been waiting for the right moment to talk to you… You see, in fact…' Unflinchingly she held the keen, steady gaze of the man who was her father. She was even, in a detached way, able to spare a second to wonder if he had, at this late stage, some inkling of the truth. 'In fact, it was you I hoped to see.

'I'm sure my name didn't register properly with you—no reason why it should.' Such an effort to appear calm and at ease. 'But I was born Ginny Martyn-Browne and I understand you and my…my parents were very good friends when you were in Hong Kong.'

Hugo Vanbrugh stared—it was obvious to her that he was shocked, possibly even angry. In the background she was aware of Jake telling his mother of her unexpected appearance in his office, of Karen's reluctance to admit her...

'Martyn-Browne, you say?' Hugo had regained his composure. 'Ah, that I do remember. I met Tom at the military hospital; he fixed up a broken tooth.' Ah, so they had met, Ginny thought, but did not say anything. 'I remember them both very well.'

It was a relief to hear Jake take up the story. 'Apparently Ginny's parents had this plan to come to the States to look you up—that's right, isn't it, Ginny?'

'Yes, but my father died two years ago.' It was so painful to recall, especially in these fraught circumstances.

'Oh, I'm sorry about that. And...your mother?' Hugo Vanbrugh paused. 'Jane, wasn't it?'

Something about that hesitation, that hint of vagueness, struck at Ginny. Suppose she was all wrong? That it hadn't been the love affair of the century? Suppose her mother had been one in a succession of Hugo Vanbrugh's women and he *really* had a problem thinking of her name? Her voice shook dangerously. 'She...she was killed in a traffic accident several months ago.'

'Oh, my dear.' Mrs Vanbrugh reached out a comforting hand. 'How terribly sad for you.'

'Mmm.' She played with a fork until her composure was regained. 'Anyway, since I had to come to New York on a quick business trip—' that lie came easily and might be useful if she were forced to extricate herself hurriedly '—and since I knew it was my parents' plan, I decided on the spur of the moment to look you up, though I had no intention of gatecrashing the way I seem to have done.' Ignoring the murmurs of dissent, she went on. 'There are one or two mementoes they planned to let you have.'

'Well, I'm sorry about your father, Ginny, he was a fine man. And your mother too; I remember she was a formidable opponent at the bridge table. A wonderful woman.' A faint smile did not wholly disguise Hugo's shocked expression, but whether that signified distress at the news or merely concern about its implications on his own life it was impossible to say.

'Yes, she was still that, right to the end of her life.' Though her voice wobbled again, Ginny was able to smile with a touch of defiance, unaware that her strained expression revealed damaged emotions. 'She was so active, so full of life...' She bit at her lower lip then continued. 'But here am I, casting a blight on what has been such a wonderful day.' A more genuine smile now as she raised an almost empty glass. 'Once again, congratulations and very best wishes.'

The older couple murmured appreciatively and a moment later Mrs Vanbrugh spoke reflectively. 'You mustn't apologise, Ginny, it does us good to think of other people at such times. And to consider that not everyone has been as fortunate as we have. But one thing you must remember: your parents were very fortunate to have a daughter like you. They must have been so proud.'

It took a considerable effort of will to avoid flicking a glance in Hugo's direction, although she knew he was watching her intently. Most likely he was trying to decide exactly why she was here—blackmail might be one of the possibilities which would occur to him, and serve him right!

But she smiled at his wife with what serenity she could muster. 'You are very kind. And of course it worked both ways, I had the best of parents.' Let him remember that when I put him in the picture completely, she prayed mutinously. 'I was lucky in my relationship with them.'

After that the conversation became general. Mrs Vanbrugh swept Ginny out through the French doors and down the flight of steps to the paved area about the pool, demonstrating her passion for gardening as they went by naming all the climbing roses and shrubs which rioted colourfully over the surrounding walls. Then they went out through a wrought-iron gate, took a short stroll across the park and came back into the house through the main entrance.

'Now, my dear.' Inside the hallway Mrs Vanbrugh paused, apologising with a sigh. 'Would you mind terribly if I begged to be allowed to go to bed?' She flashed Ginny a beguiling smile. 'It has been a hectic day and I feel quite tired—and…more champagne than I'm used to.'

'More than most people are used to, I imagine, and of course I don't mind. It would be more surprising if you weren't exhausted.' She was about to say she would like to do the same when Jake appeared, his father close on his heels.

'I've got to go out. I hope you don't mind.' Jake's explanation was offered to both women but directed more to Ginny. 'There's some trouble with Randy; Miguel just called.' He was moving towards the door.

'But don't go to bed, Ginny. I thought we might have a swim later... I'll see you before you go to sleep, Mother.' And, before anyone could reply, he was taking the steps two at a time in his easy, athletic stride. Seconds later a vehicle accelerated down the drive.

His mother stood, one foot resting on the lowest tread of the staircase. 'Randy is the first stallion Jake had, but he's getting to be an old fellow now. Miguel is the head groom and he has been worried, anxious for Jake to take a look at him. Anyway, I don't suppose he'll be long.' She swung round towards her husband. 'I'm going to bed, darling.' He came across, put an arm about her waist and kissed her cheek.

'I'll see you soon.'

'Oh.' She had just begun to climb the stairs when she obviously had a thought. 'Isn't this the perfect time for your chat with Ginny? You won't have time in the morning. Go on—you can both reminisce like mad and...didn't you say something about a memento, my dear?'

'Yes.' Now that the moment was upon her, Ginny found herself trembling. 'In fact—' she determined to be positive '—I'll run up now and pick up the package.'

Having said goodnight to her hostess, she paused inside the spacious bedroom, barely aware of the elegant pink drapes, the soft patina of old colonial furniture. Then, with a sigh, she moved forward, retrieved the taped package from the drawer where she had put it earlier and was about to leave when she caught sight of herself in the cheval-glass.

Surprising that after such a traumatic day she

should look so comparatively normal. None of her friends, if they could see her now, would have guessed she was passing through one of the most testing times of her life. Her eyes were softly luminous, cheeks delicately flushed, mouth apparently ready to curve into a smile, but it was all at odds with her quivering nerves.

At least, she assured herself, Hugo Vanbrugh needn't be ashamed of their relationship, and she blessed the forethought which had prompted her to pack one of her prettiest summer outfits. The silk T-shirt was in her favourite amber colour and she had teamed it with a shortish sarong-style skirt, black, but scribbled all over with topaz. It shrieked 'Paris' and gave wonderful exposure to her long shapely legs.

She loved wearing it, and if it wasn't for her present predicament... She took a moment to brush her hair into a floating nimbus, gave herself a brief spray of perfume, another French extravagance, and then, in a wild urge to get things over, she hurried from the room.

'Come through here, Ginny.' He must have been waiting for her, and led her along a corridor to the back of the house. 'We shan't be disturbed.'

They were in an obviously male retreat, much darker and more austere than the rest of the house, with much wood panelling, sporting prints and antique guns. He gestured towards a green leather chair, deeply buttoned, and sat in the matching one on the far side of the fireplace sighing deeply.

'Now perhaps we can get down to some explanations...'

In spite of her deep agitation, Ginny forced herself to look directly into his eyes. After all, she had done nothing to be ashamed of and had no intention of embarrassing him. In fact, she seemed to be the one who would suffer most from the whole confused affair. A sob began in her throat but she choked it back.

'Before I go on, I want to say how sorry I am that your family is involved. That was the last thing I intended should happen. As explained, I went to your office, asked for you and found myself talking to Jake. After that I seemed to lose control of the situation—Jake simply railroaded me.'

That brought a wry grin to Hugo's mouth. 'I can believe that.'

He waited for her to continue, and she found all the little speeches she had prepared simply stuck in her throat—for how to explain to a man that he was looking at a daughter whose existence he had never suspected? The result of a long-abandoned liaison which he scarcely remembered. Was there a painless way to break such news? If there was then she wished she could find it, but...

'Perhaps it would be better if I were to give you this letter to read first.'

She watched him frown over his own name on the envelope—when he caught his breath did it mean he'd recognised the handwriting? Then he extracted the pages and began to scan the lines, one clenched fist pressed hard against his forehead. That was when Ginny had to avert her face. Once or twice he murmured her mother's name, but in a voice so distraught she wished she could stop her ears.

She had been wrong! So wrong to seek peace for herself at someone else's expense. Her own self-interest could not only have repercussions for Hugo but could seriously damage his family. And not only the Vanbrughs. Knowing that soon she would have to leave Jake... Maybe that would be a fitting retribution—certainly it brought a sorrow which was beyond tears.

Hugo had finished reading. The hand holding the pages drooped, and it was a long time before the silence was broken with a desolate sigh. 'So, Ginny...what you are saying...'

She raised her head, saw dark, slender fingers rake through the silvery hair and was filled with pity for the man who was going through such a cataclysmic reappraisal.

'It was just as shattering for me. I never had the least suspicion that Tom—I loved him so much—that he wasn't my real father.' Pain meant that she was unable to say more.

'Wouldn't...?' There was a trace of bitterness in his voice. He rose, walked past her to the window. 'Wouldn't it have been better to leave things as they were?'

'Maybe.' Foolish to feel so wounded. It was especially wounding that he was confirming her own immediate thoughts. 'Only, there was so much passion, such intensity in everything my mother wrote—I felt a tremendous compulsion, for her sake as much as my own. You were so obviously the love of her life...'

'And she of mine.' His voice was ragged. His sincerity could not be doubted. He crossed the room and sat down again. 'I'm sorry, Ginny, the last thing I ought to do is blame you for anything.' His smile was brief and tortured. 'It's just…so…so shocking to think that Jane…that you…'

'One way I feel I am to blame is how I went about things. There are more discreet ways I ought to have chosen. I could have approached you through a third party—I know very well it could have been done. Instead I rushed over here thinking I could manage it all myself and… Well, you need never worry that I shall say a word to anyone else. You and I are the only two people in the world who need ever know…'

'Thank you for that. I would hate if Marion were to find out, though…she did know there was someone. Maybe I'd better explain…' He gave a heavy sigh.

'We met and married as soon as I graduated from West Point, but almost at once she realised she didn't like life as an army wife. It was my chosen career, which I loved, but I found it hard going about on my own.

'Marion stayed here in the family home with her parents. All her friends were close by and she loved being on the ranch with her horses. By the time I went to Nam we had been living apart, except for furloughs. Maybe even drifting apart. And then I met Jane when I was in Hong Kong…'

There was a longish silence when it seemed he might have forgotten Ginny's presence, the deep-set eyes reflecting a mix of happiness and pain.

'Well…' He came to with a little shrug. 'I can't explain except to say that I fell desperately in love

with her—something I'd had no experience of at that
level—and for Jane it was the same. If she had agreed
to divorce Tom I would have left Marion, we would
have married eventually and…how different life
might have been for…well, for all of us. But you must
know your mother had very committed principles, and
nothing I could say would persuade her. And, apart
from that, she couldn't bear to hurt your father.' As
he used that word he frowned, grimaced slightly in
pained apology. 'You can see as much from the letter.'

'Yes.' Suffused by a wholly unexpected wave of
sympathy for him, Ginny resisted the urge to put out
a comforting hand. He was not the kind of man to
welcome such gestures. 'Yes, I can see that.'

'In the end your father—' he gave a faintly grim
smile as he corrected the slip this time '—I mean *Tom*
was due back. Things were building up in Vietnam
and we decided to break things off. As it happened, I
got wounded pretty badly, came back on a stretcher
and had a long spell of recuperation.

'I tried to accept what Jane had decided, though I
won't pretend it was easy. I went through many dark,
bitter nights. We had agreed to have no further contact
and that was pretty hard—though it might have been
for the best.

'Marion and I agreed to try to save our marriage
for everyone's sake, for there was Jake to consider as
well. I made up my mind to quit the service so we
could have a more regular lifestyle and I set up my
own company.

'That, at least, has been a great success. The hard

work in the early days might have helped take my mind off the personal problems and Marion was invaluable on the social side and... Well, we've been happy for the last twenty or so years.'

'I think everyone who sees you will know that.'

'As she said, we've been lucky. I've been more than lucky to have had...' His voice trailed away as he withdrew into his own thoughts and Ginny sat quietly, dreaming her own dreams, coming back to the present when she felt his eyes, colouring up when she met his quizzical expression.

'One thing Marion said tonight—I want you to know how much I agree. Your parents were—oh, God—*are* very proud of you.'

'Oh...' Again she felt shaken, longing to weep.

'And I'm sorry if at first I was discouraging. It all came as something of a shock, to hear the name and then...' He looked down at the letter he was still holding. 'And then to learn that, in contradiction of everything I've believed, I have a daughter.'

'It must be strange.' The build-up of emotions she dared not show was almost overwhelming, and in an attempt at diversion she reached out for the other things her mother had kept. She extracted a small painting. 'This—I'm not sure if it means anything to you, but...I see Mother painted it.' A finger touched the initials in one corner. 'It's just possible the ''J'' could be taken for a ''T'', so conceivably my father Tom could have painted it. They were both arty.'

'This...' His voice shook, was very low. 'This is the view from the balcony of our hotel. Where we spent the last few days.' And where her life had actually begun. Ginny was surprised by the power of her own emotions.

'And here…I'm sure you'll recognise them—are two American cap badges, and one or two photographs—though…I don't think I can identify either of you.'

'Ah, that was a mess function. I remember one or two faces, but the names… Long since gone.'

'And I brought a photograph—one of the last taken of my parents together.' Ginny handed over the snapshot, saw his face contort as he recognised Jane.

'Ah… Ah, yes. She…she had hardly changed, except perhaps to grow more beautiful, and Tom…well, I hardly remember him. We met so briefly.'

'I'm sorry.' Impulsively, forgetting her initial restraint, she leaned forward and touched his hand. 'Sorry to bring you so much pain, but for myself— I can't say I regret coming. Not even if I was quite wrong.'

'Of course you weren't wrong.' Rising, he placed a hand on her shoulder. 'I know as well as anyone how powerful—' From outside the sound of voices caused him to break off. 'Anyway, I think Jake is back and… You know that Marion and I leave tomorrow?'

'Yes, Jake did say. A cruise, isn't it?'

'Yes. All rather badly arranged. Originally it was scheduled for next week, but the sailing date was changed so… It's all been too much of a rush. We sail to Hawaii then on to Singapore.'

'Thank you for being so understanding.'

'Thank you for having the courage. And, you

know, when we get back home—' He broke off again
as the door opened and Jake stood there.

'Have you had your talk, then?'

'Yes.' It was an effort to act normally but Ginny
managed a smile. 'Mission accomplished. I've done
what I set out to do.'

'And I was just about to suggest, Jake, that she stay
on here for a day or two, to keep you company.'

'Oh, I don't think...' It was important to nip this
idea in the bud. 'I snatched only a few days' leave...'

'Well...' Jake held the door open. 'I'm going to
snatch you off for a swim now. The moon is coming
up and when you see that...' As he spoke Jake pulled
loose his tie and began to unbutton his shirt. 'So, I'll
meet you in the hall in five minutes.

'Oh.' He turned back. 'I saw Mother—she's almost
asleep.'

'Yes, I'm just going.' Hugo spoke to his son's re-
treating back, then to Ginny. 'You'll give me time to
think about all this?'

'As far as I'm concerned, the matter is finished.
I've done what I wanted to do and now I feel life will
return to something like normal. As soon as I can, I'm
going back to London to get on with my life.'

'Thank you, Ginny. And I shall be in contact.' He
smiled, and for a moment she could see just what had
attracted her mother so powerfully. 'Now off you go
and enjoy your swim.'

CHAPTER FOUR

How could she? How *could* she enjoy her swim when her mind was teeming with so many contrary impressions? That the rhetorical question was inconsistent with her actions as she struggled into her bikini did not occur to her.

Her New York hotel had been advertised as having its own pool, which was why she had brought it with her, but it would have been perfectly easy to deny its existence. Only... She brushed the hair back from her face with half-amused cynicism... Only, she loved to swim—spent much of her spare time in the pool at her club—finding it the perfect way to relax after a stressful day. And the interview with Hugo...

But, enjoy herself? No chance. *Mend* herself. That would be more to the point. A blouse was draped about her shoulders, feet thrust into sandals, and she ran down the staircase, out of the side door and into the garden.

And what a place to unwind. At first she thought she had the garden and pool to herself—perfect, as far as she was concerned, for the ambience could hardly have been improved. The scented air was like silk against her skin and the full moon sailing above massive treetops had touched everything with silver.

She held her breath. She walked forward, tossing her blouse in the direction of a lounger, enjoying the touch of cool tiles against her feet, toes curling round the edge as she prepared to dive. Then, in the shadow of the rose arbour, something moved. Jake came slowly towards her.

Determined to be unaware of him, she tried to be unmoved by so much male perfection—wide, bronzed shoulders, narrow hips clad in dark trunks, long, powerful legs which were no surprise since she knew, from the dinner conversation, that he was a keen sportsman. But what *misery* that she must not *allow* herself to dwell... The professional woman in her strove to stay detached.

'I was beginning to think you had changed your mind.' There was amusement in the deep voice, forcing her onto the defensive. She could not allow him to find her in the least bit nervous... Or even to suspect a guilty secret...

'Now, why should you think that?'

'Oh.'

The amazing eyes had a black, silvery glitter in this light and were absorbing detail, making her regret that she had lingered on the edge. If she had dived beneath the surface...

Now his attention was on her hair which was surely in disarray. His gaze moved in a leisurely way across her face...shoulders...body...legs. She was irritated with herself that her reaction was so warm—where was all the detachment she had promised herself seconds ago?—but pleased that she was looking good.

Her legs had always been long and slender, her figure not too bad—certainly this navy polka-dot bikini was flattering, if a bit on the scanty side. She caught fiercely at her revealing thoughts—come to think of it, how much better if she had been a head shorter in the circumstances—and maybe fifty pounds heavier, or…

'Oh, I thought…fatigue…or some other reason,' he said mockingly.

'Well, you could have a point, but the prospect of a moonlight swim…' He'd better believe that, she thought. And, in an effort to bring the matter to a close, she turned and with a neat running dive broke the surface of the water.

She began a steady, powerful crawl, and realised at once that she was being paced. After several lengths, knowing escape was impossible, she paused, leaned against the end rail and settled into a half-seated posture, allowing her feet to float while he trod water, looking at her.

'What a perfect night.' Her face was raised to the heavens. 'So warm and beautiful.'

'We have lots of nights like this in Virginia.' The pitch of his voice was a blatant invitation to flirtation.

'So.' She allowed him a casual, amused glance. 'I hope you count your blessings.'

'Oh, I do,' he assured her with mocking humility. 'Every last one, Miss Ginny.'

'Idiot,' she laughed, splashing him with water.

'No, seriously.' He joined her at the rail. 'I do know how lucky I've been.' Then he reached out, twisted a lock of her sodden hair. 'You ought to have worn a cap. You'll be up until all hours drying it.'

'Hmm. I forgot to bring one. I'd imagined a decorous little dip in the hotel pool instead…'

'Instead of the abandoned time we're having here?'

'Well, I wouldn't have put it in those terms.' Refusing to look at him directly, she found herself nevertheless forced to exercise iron control. 'Pleasant. Relaxing, perhaps, rather than abandoned.'

It was a mistake to repeat that last word when the mental images were so disturbing—his hair sleek against his head like a black cap, the broad chest with its scatter of dark hair and... The thought of touching it with her fingertips was so arousing... 'But, I admit, it has much more going for it than a dingy hotel pool.'

Her pushed himself away from the side, 'Well, come on. Another few lengths and then I invite you to hot chocolate and cookies in the kitchen.'

'Oh, I think bed, don't you?'

'And then bed. I'm not suggesting an all-night rave.'

'I do realise that.' She replied a trifle sharply. Why did he persist with his efforts to distract?

'Is there a hair-drier in your room?'

'I don't know, but in any case I have my own with me. It won't take long...'

'Right.' They had reached the end near the house and he stood watching as she climbed from the pool, pausing at the top to hitch the strap of her bikini. 'You go on in and dry your hair. I shall meet you in the hall in twenty minutes.'

'I'm not sure—' she began, but he had swum off before she had time to inform him that, in fact, she *was* sure—quite sure—she would not be taking him up on his offer.

Even after a swift shower and hair-rinsing session,

when she sat in front of the dressing-table mirror wielding the drier, she was resolute. For one thing she really was tired—physically, at least. Emotionally she felt as if she were on some sort of high. Scarcely surprising since it had been a hectic day in every sense.

Her dried hair was looking its best—soft and bouncy, gleaming with highlights. And yet, what was the harm? When it was the one thing in the world she wanted to do, and when she knew the score, where was the harm?

Very soon she would be back in London and the memories would have to last for the rest of her life. She was entitled to some memories, for heaven's sake. Rather like her mother in that respect, now she thought of it. Except that Jane had had glorious, vivid memories, whereas she could never...

No! *No!* She was shocked by the way her mind was betraying her.

But, in any case, she now knew that what she felt for Jake was liking, nothing more. A strong liking, certainly, but that probably had a great deal to do with their inherited genes. She had, in the past, met several men whom she had liked as much—well, *almost* as much as Jake Vanbrugh—it was simply this special situation which gave everything an extra edge.

Reassured by that knowledge, she sighed her relief and reached out for her kaftan, which she pulled on over her short nightie. Then a quick spray of Givenchy perfume and she was running down the curving staircase before she had time to think of an opposing theory.

It was only when she caught sight of Jake, appearing from the direction of the kitchen, that she became more circumspect. She must remember that he was in total ignorance. Putting one hand on the balustrade, she slowed down. He paused when he caught sight of her, watching as she took the last few steps, a faint smile curving his mouth as she stood in front of him.

'So.' The warmth in his voice brought surging excitement to her chest. She was perversely pleased when his glance took in all the shimmering peacock colours of her floor-length robe. 'I wondered if perhaps you would change your mind...'

Best to be severe—to cool her own imagination if for no other reason. 'As I recall, I was given very little choice. Any protest I made was swept aside.'

'Which makes you the perfect guest,' he teased, before propelling her with a touch on the elbow through a door and into the kitchen which, although obviously high tech, was very much antebellum in style.

A large oak table and chairs were in the centre of the floor, with various dressers round the walls—one displaying blue and white china, another filled with copper cooking pots. An arch led to an annexe where an enormous electric cooker, refrigerator and freezer, all white and gleaming, ruled supreme. And here was another dresser, displaying an assortment of simple pottery, most in a dark reddish clay. She leaned forward to examine them more easily.

'Those are early American redware pieces—the everyday dishes used by the first settlers. Extremely common at one time, so therefore little valued. Now, though, they are becoming quite collectable.'

'Interesting.' Ginny turned, seeing the room from a different angle. The flagstoned floor was very much the colour of the dishes, dark terracotta, but with a modern treatment which gave it a soft gleam. Here and there peg rugs were scattered, with a very large one in front of the fireplace, which was a large inglenook where flames were flickering.

'Not the real thing.' Jake indicated that she should take one of the rocking chairs flanking the fireplace. As she did so she was given a long brass toasting fork, and a bowl of marshmallows was put on a nearby table. 'The fire, I mean. When the house was built logs would have burned here day and night, but now the fire is part of the heating system—on and off at the touch of a switch. But it's fine for toasting marshmallow, so, if you'd like to start, I'll go and see to the hot chocolate.'

'This is a job.' She frowned, concentrating as she introduced the sweetmeat to the fork. 'One I've never done before.'

'No? Well, with your training, you can surely cope.' The gentle irony made her smile as she lay back against the cushions, extending bare feet to the flames, watching a wisp of sugary smoke begin to rise. Behind her, from the annexe, there were the sounds of china clinking, water boiling and being poured. It was all so comfortably domestic.

Then he was back, taking up the conversation where it had been left. 'This is one of the things I remember from when I was a kid. We'd spend a winter's afternoon tobogganing, then we'd come back here for hot drinks and toast.' He sat opposite, and she watched intently as the strong planes of his face were illuminated by the flickering firelight. The little half-smile and the gleam in his eyes indicated how happy those days had been. Then he shot a swift glance towards her. 'I suppose you did that too.'

'Not that, specifically.' Unexpectedly she was enveloped in a wave of sheer resentment—this ought to have been *her* background, these *her* memories, not simply ones to be enjoyed vicariously. Why had she missed out on so much? Her mother too. It was unfair…

Guilt took over then. How could she have even a second's regret when her parents had been everything loving parents could be…? 'But we had many other happy times,' she said firmly. She took the large cup he was offering. 'Mmm.' It was heavy and needed two hands as she carefully replaced it on the saucer. 'Quite delicious.'

Ginny nibbled on a cookie, then, as directed, dropped one of the toasted mallows into the cup and drank through it. 'Help!' She licked the froth from her upper lip, smiling as Jake handed her a tissue.

Lying back in his chair, he seemed content to watch her. His legs, clad in dark cotton, were stretched out to the blaze, pale silk shirt open at the throat. She marvelled, not for the first time, that she had allowed this man to dictate to her, to undermine her judgements with such ease, but…

They were so insidious, all her feelings. So novel, demolishing all her decisions. Worry began to gnaw at her again. She raised the cup to her mouth then replaced it with the kind of thump which might have been a statement.

'Jake.' Now she looked away from him, though she sensed her tone had made his eyes narrow. 'I *must* think about getting back to New York. Do you know anything about flights? I thought tomorrow…'

'I thought we would go back together—as we came down.' Under the contemplative tone she sensed irritation which she felt she ought to deflect. The last thing she wanted was open disagreement.

'Well, of course, you know—you must know—and I've said it before—travelling by private jet is much more comfortable in every way…'

'Really?'

Now she did look. And though he was unsmiling she caught a touch of humour.

'I was beginning to think this determination to travel commercial meant you had misgivings about the pilot.'

'You must know better than that.' Time to be light-hearted, even slightly crushing—she imagined that he was not the kind of man who came across that reaction too often. 'I made quite sure you did not see my crossed fingers during take-off and landing.'

'No.' He was perfectly straight-faced. 'I was unaware of the crossed fingers, but I could see your feet firmly pressed on the floor as you tried to brake.'

'Now that,' she began indignantly, 'is completely untrue.' Then, when he laughed, she joined in with a little reluctance. 'I had total confidence in you as a

pilot. So there. And I didn't mean to tell you that.
But, to get back to the journey...'

'Well, tomorrow is going to be rather awkward.
The parents are going to Washington so the jet will
be in use...'

'Are you taking them there?'

'No. Dad is piloting the plane himself and someone
will fly it back here, so if you'll have a little pa-
tience... Besides—' now his expression was more
cautious '—I have plans for us.'

'You have?' She raised what she hoped was a scep-
tical eyebrow. 'But since the whole purpose of my
visit has been accomplished...'

'Ah, yes. I was meaning to ask, how was your
chat?'

'With *your* father?' She groaned inwardly. Why
had she put even the faintest emphasis on that word,
as if she were issuing a disclaimer? But at least he
appeared not to have noticed. She gave a shaky smile.
'At least he didn't seem to think I was behaving too
foolishly. And he was glad of the few mementoes.
Yes...' Her smile grew a shade more determined. 'I
think I can say the trip has been a success.'

'Then why not make it even more of a success?
After the parents leave tomorrow I mean to ride some
of the estate boundaries. Why don't you come with
me and enjoy one of the most beautiful parts of the
United States?'

'Oh...'

'You do ride, I hope?'

'Yes, but...'

'Come *on*. You can't fly thousands of miles for just a day or two.'

She felt like the drowning man clutching at straws. 'Well, as I said, I have one or two other things to see to in New York—and as for flying thousands of miles for a brief stay, I'm sure you do that all the time.'

'Yes.' Did the knowing look in his eyes signal confidence that she was about to concede? 'I have little choice. But you... All you have to do is pick up the telephone and call Mr. Brockway. I'm sure he'll say whatever Miss Browne wants...'

'In which case I shall be very much surprised.'

'Yes?'

'Very. Since Mr Brockway has been dead these forty years I should be surprised if he said anything much at all, let alone granted extended leave to a junior employee.'

He grinned, and shrugged indulgently. 'Well, whoever... Now, why don't we sit here for an hour or two? Speaking for myself, I can imagine nothing better.' His lips pursed in qualification. 'At least, there's *almost* nothing I would rather do than sit here with you drinking hot chocolate, toasting marshmallows while you tell me the story of your life. And then you can ring up your London office and suggest that a few extra days would not be unreasonable.'

'Mmm.' She recognised a warning when she met one, and that slight but deliberate implication as to how he would be even more inclined to spend his time was not lost on Ginny. She had met it before, but never in the past had she felt so threatened. And simply thinking about that was frightening— Because this was the first time she had had the inclination to respond.

Inclination! The word almost brought a wry smile—as if this burning, surging longing could be described by such a feeble word. It was necessary to put on an act. She rose, stretching lazily, smothering a tiny yawn. 'Oh! Much as I would like to sit chatting, Jake, I must go to bed before I nod off in the chair.'

'If you must.' Rising, he walked with her to the door before pausing, one hand on the knob. She looked up at him, moist lips slightly parted, eyes luminous.

'Goodnight, Jake.' Her voice was soft, possibly more encouraging than she knew—soft and encouraging and tender. And maybe it was in reaction to it that his hand came out and lightly touched her hair before his fingers curved about the nape of her neck.

The sensation brought fear, stark and unmistakable, boiling up inside her. Wide-eyed she stared up, heart pounding, wild pulses beating in her throat.

'Ginny...' A man's eyes had never been so mesmerising, so compelling. 'You can't imagine how glad I am that you came.' A finger moved against sensitive skin, began to diminish her fear, to encourage the softer, more compliant emotions.

'Can't I?' Meant to be cool, moody, the words were somehow translated into a coquettish query, suggesting that perhaps she *could* imagine...

'Mmm.' It was a long, sighing comment as his hand slipped lower, pulling her against him. 'I doubt anyone can.'

If she had been sensible she would have stretched

up to drop a casual, sisterly kiss on his cheek; she would have assured him that she, too, was glad—delighted, in fact—that chance had brought her here, that she could never have dreamed…et cetera…et cetera.

But at that moment common sense had been wiped from Ginny Browne's agenda. All her moral determination had evaporated the moment he put a finger beneath her chin, raising her face to his. It was complete capitulation, with her lips parted in eager welcome.

Later, lying in the coolness of her wide bed, she found it difficult to forgive or even to understand her behaviour. She replayed the scene as it *ought* to have unfolded.

In her repertoire of courtroom approaches she had perfected the exact tone—agreeable, friendly, but subtly detached. 'I value so much this opportunity to experience American life at close quarters,' she should have said. 'I shall always be grateful to your parents for making it possible.'

That would have been a nice touch, though one which would have been lost on him for obvious reasons. Then she should have given a last, lingering glance round the kitchen, as if she were indeed a tourist taking a departing look at a stately house. 'Goodnight, Jake,' she should have said. 'And thank you. Thank you all.'

But of course she had said and done none of those things. Instead, she had behaved with a degree of irresponsibility which was little short of criminal: Falling into his arms, rejoicing in his power and then allowing herself to be pulled into the curve of his body—even reaching an arm about his neck, extending her fingers to lace through the dark hair, so incredibly soft and silky. Moving her body in a way that was deliberately provocative.

In those first delirious moments, when his lips— brushing, teasing, then at last dominating and possessing—had been dropping kisses through her hair, butterfly touches on eyelids and down her cheeks, when his hands had been moulding her body against his, she had felt herself drowning in pure sensual pleasure...

But memory had flooded back with brutal immediacy. The enormity of her behaviour had suddenly had her reeling with self-disgust. The hand which had been lying against his chest in a yielding, very nearly submissive way had suddenly been geared to rejection—except...how to explain such contradictory behaviour? One moment total indiscretion, the next an outraged Victorian Miss.

Her mind had raced with the effort of defusing a situation unlike any other she had encountered. Above all, she'd told herself, she must be firm, she must act as if this bewildering interlude had never happened.

Certainly it ought not to have done, if she'd had the wit to stick to her original intention of going to bed.

In the end she had given a heartfelt sigh tinged with a little regret and then backed away, contriving a faint smile, and shrugging. 'As I said a long time ago, Jake. Bed, I think.'

He'd been lit by a flicker from the hearth, standing

utterly still—certainly making no effort to detain her. But his attention had been so concentrated that it was as if he would deny her the right to her own decision. His chest had been rising and falling with the same haste with which she had been striving to control herself. An odd expression had been in his eyes—impenetrable but somehow chilling...frustration? If he was suffering that why should she be surprised? She, at last, had some idea of what that could mean. He had spoken, forcing her to recall exactly how ill-chosen her last words had been.

'Is that...an invitation, Ginny?'

For a second her mind was blank, then was swamped by a wave of hideous embarrassment mixed with anger, both of which, she was certain would be noted. Her tiny laugh was sheer affectation, but it helped her through her real anguish, her longing to shout out, Yes, yes, it is an invitation if you want to accept it! And, of course, that would have been his cue for sweeping her off her feet and bounding up the staircase two steps at a time.

But she was carefully languid as she took a step towards the door. 'I think we inhabit different worlds, Jake. A casual goodnight kiss is definitely not an automatic invitation to play bedroom games in my book.' She marvelled that she could sound so experienced.

'If that was a casual goodnight kiss then we *do* inhabit different worlds.' His lazy half-smile did nothing to disguise his flashing anger. 'And I suggest you choose your words with more care after this.'

'Don't lecture me.' Frustration made her adopt the tone of a sharp-tongued magistrate. 'If you recall, I've been suggesting bed—*my* bed, for me alone—for *hours*. But you have kept…' Her brain was searching for an elusive word but he was the one who produced it, in the light-hearted, teasing way she found particularly infuriating.

'*Propositioning* you?' In spite of the raised eyebrow and the wicked gleam he was trying to project an air of innocent detachment.

'I was *not* going to say that.' Halfway between tears and hysteria, dismayed by her urge to ridicule both of them for the farcical situation they had brought upon themselves, she pursed her lips. ' "Tempting" was the word I was looking for.'

'Ah?' A wealth of innuendo in that simple word. 'And what about tomorrow and my prop—my suggestion, my *tempting* suggestion that you should stay on here for another day or two?'

'Ah…' she began, in mocking parody, and was foolishly pleased by his flicker of appreciation at her imitation. 'I shall have to sleep on that one. Goodnight, Jake.'

And she had swept from the kitchen with the comfortable feeling of having had the last word. But still without the slightest idea of how she meant to answer his question.

CHAPTER FIVE

THE following day was one Ginny knew she would remember till the end of her life—so golden and sun-drenched, as relaxed and happy as a day remembered from childhood, without the tiniest flaw. It was sheer perfection.

She was downstairs in time to see Marion and Hugo depart in a mass of luggage, was enveloped by the woman and kissed warmly, as if she were an old and valued family friend. Hugo's embrace, when his wife had got into the car, was more restrained, but he took the opportunity for a few private words.

'When we return from the cruise I shall be in touch with you, Ginny. And...and thank you for having the courage to come. It can't have been easy for you.'

Conscious of Jake arranging cases nearby, she determined to be casual. 'Thank you for taking it as you did. It must have been a devastating shock for you.'

'That, certainly.' His smile was a little taut. 'But, once I absorb the facts, I'm sure it will bring nothing but pleasure.'

That was something she doubted, but nevertheless the sentiment was touching. Now it was time to divert the conversation. 'It must be wonderful for you both to have the chance to get away...'

'Mmm. Should be interesting.' He threw a quick glance over his shoulder towards Jake, who was having a final word with Marion. Hugo's voice was lowered, his manner almost furtive. 'Ginny, there's something I must explain to you. I'm not sure how much you and Jake feel...'

'Don't give me away, Dad.' His son came up behind him, draped an arm about his father's shoulder.

'Jake.' The older man smiled, albeit with a touch of reluctance. 'I didn't hear you come up.'

'Obviously.' Jake grinned mischievously. 'But I won't have you spilling the beans about me; you ought to be on my side.'

'Well, now Ginny will never hear what a truly wonderful person you are.' He reached down for the document case at his feet, searched in a pocket and produced a bunch of keys. 'No, what I was about to say was that Marion and I hoped Ginny would stay on with you for a few days. You've been working nonstop for months, and I dare say Ginny is under similar pressure. Now—' he handed his case to his son '—put that in the car, will you? Then we must be off.'

A moment later he had turned to his daughter, speaking softly but with some urgency. 'Ginny, there's still so much we have to say to each other. We need an hour or two of peace and quiet, and for that I shall come to London as soon as I can and... Thanks, Jake, now we really must go. Marion's looking impatient.'

And, moments later, Jake and Ginny saw the vehicle disappear round a bend in the drive *en route* for the private runway. Then they walked inside the kitchen, where they sat at the table and he began to pour coffee.

It was a moment or two before he spoke. 'Well, you have decided to stay.' It was more a statement than a question and one she had an urge to contradict. She wasn't a child, to have her decisions made for her, her plans changed. When she had got out of bed this morning she had known what she had to do, and simply because Hugo had suggested…

'Jake.' Trying to convey conviction, she rose and indicated the short navy skirt, the white blouse tied at the neck by a pink scarf. 'Do I look as if I'm dressed for the country? This is my New York outfit; I did tell you I meant to go back today.'

'It'll take you only minutes to change into jeans and a T-shirt. I'm sure I can find something to fit if you haven't brought any.'

'Jake.' In her irritation she spoke through her teeth. 'Why do you have to be so…so…?' Unable to find the appropriate word she ended weakly, 'So masculine?' Immediately she undermined her protest with a little giggle while he appeared to consider.

'It's a good question. But I'm not sure I'm the best person to answer.'

'I didn't mean that. In fact, I can't think what I meant.'

'Your apology is accepted.'

Her sigh of irritation was ignored and he rose, came round the table and placed his hands on her shoulders, giving her a tiny shake. 'And I promise you, I shall never complain that I find you too…' he frowned in comical parody '…too…what's the word? Ah, yes, too feminine. And now go and get ready—I'll take you on a grand tour of the Vanbrugh estate.'

And it was rather dismaying to find how obediently she did that. In moments she had thrown off her city clothes, pulled on some jeans and a checked shirt and had run down as if that had been her plan all along. Still, she thought, subduing her doubts, it was what Hugo had advised. And she had the feeling that if she were to protest any more Jake might become suspicious, start putting two and two together. Something which, in view of her promises to her father, she dare not risk.

They were soon in the pick-up truck, driving round to the stables, 'Now I can tell you how pleased I am that you decided to stay on.' The note of blatant satisfaction caused fresh waves of exasperation in Ginny.

'I think the decision was made *for* me. If I had done as *I* preferred I would be on my way to New York by now.' Then, having made her point, she felt a stab of guilt. 'But, on the other hand, most people would say that all the advantages are on my side.'

All her irritation was forgotten when they were mounted, riding across the parkland on that glorious sunny morning. It was impossible to hide her pleasure. Rising in the stirrups, she patted her filly's neck. 'She's a lovely girl.'

'She's one of Randy's offspring.'

Recalling the dark chestnut stallion left back at the stables, Ginny frowned. 'It's hard to believe there's any connection.'

'An accidental covering.' He held back an overhanging branch. 'A coquettish mare broke into his compound. Lucy is the result.'

'Oh?' Best not to dwell on certain similarities with

her own situation. 'Miguel is concerned? About Randy, I mean?'

'Yes, the old fellow's losing ground. At one time he would have snatched at that apple you offered, but today...' He gave a despondent shrug. 'He's frustrated, used to being ridden hard, and he can't accept that he's no longer fit enough. But who knows? He might improve. He's a fighter and never gives up easily.'

'You've had him since you were a boy, your mother said.'

'Yes, we've had some great times together. But look—' the change of subject was probably deliberate '—when we climb just about to the top of this rise you'll be able to see the ocean.' He trotted ahead of her along the narrow path.

Riding the glossy black stallion, dressed in casual ranch-hand clothes, Jake seemed to her even more impressive than when she had first seen him. Following him, totally disregarding the bone-dry, slippery grass beneath them, she momentarily gave up the struggle to remain indifferent. How could she, when each time she raised her eyes there he was—in total control of the horse, powerful thighs in dark jeans, black boots with the slightly stacked heels she had seen in a dozen cowboy movies, red-and-blue-checked shirt, kerchief knotted about the dark throat?

But it was easy to make excuses for herself. She swallowed, tried to be unmoved, to view their situation as a piece of fiction. In fact, they both might have come straight out of a Western film. His role as hero was clearly cast, but she couldn't quite see where she fitted in. Saloon hostess, perhaps? Trying to adapt to life as a rancher's wife? It wouldn't be much of a return for all the hours poring over dull legal books! Fact and fiction threatened to mingle. She couldn't remember any female attorneys in Westerns...

'What's the joke, Ginny? Anything you can share?' She hadn't noticed him swing round to wait. He seemed to be sharing her amusement already, for his lips were curving in sympathy, though when she began to explain it didn't seem so funny.

'The Wild West?' There was reproach in both manner and tone. 'Most Virginians would be deeply hurt at such a suggestion.'

'Yes. And rightly so, considering we've just seen the Atlantic. But, on the other hand, you must make allowances for a Londoner.'

'Mmm.' He obviously wasn't convinced, but continued in the spirit of things. 'Anyway, a position in the Wild West for a highly qualified lawyer...?' He pondered as they ambled along. 'I'm not sure if it was possible for women to qualify in those days, but I do know it was on the frontier that American women were first emancipated.'

'Really? Isn't that surprising?'

'Surprises most people—but, when you consider, it *is* logical. The further you went west, the fewer women there were, and so they were more valued. My great-grandmother was one of the first women to be given the vote and her mother had been the only woman practising medicine in the whole of Kansas... But back to your problem. What would you say to a position on a newspaper? That would, I think, have been quite acceptable for a well brought up young woman. A lady reporter?'

'Mmm. Yes. I think I could have fitted in there. I did once think about journalism as a career.' And, chatting light-heartedly, they wandered along a sun-dappled path to the bend of a bluff where Jake slid to the ground and reached into the saddlebag for the lunch which had been prepared for them.

When they had eaten Ginny lay back with a sigh of contentment, comfortable on the soft dry vegetation, drowsy with the heat and unusual exercise, at last giving in to the temptation to close her eyes for just a moment. It was simply...irresistible.

Straightaway she was in a dream—not entirely asleep, but drifting in that delicious half-world where the impossible began to take on an aspect of probability, where... Her lips parted on a sigh of sheer longing and were brushed by...

Her eyelids flicked open and she caught the gleam of white teeth, eyes an even darker violet than... Her heart was hammering against her chest, her mind glazed with yearning, but at least she didn't panic, she congratulated herself.

'Jake!' Her voice was lazily reproving, and she flapped a hand, as if at an irritating insect, and pulled her sunglasses from her pocket and adjusted them so they afforded maximum protection. 'Jake, are you one of those irritating people who hate to see others peace-fully enjoying...?'

'It was a momentary lapse, m'lud. I don't know what came over me.' The humour faded, the intense eyes searched her features. 'Except...I can't promise not to reoffend.' He sighed deeply and lay back on one elbow. 'In any event, I thought you had slept long enough and I have so many questions I want to ask. You do realise I know very little about you—just that your father was in the army and that you might have become a journalist instead of an attorney.'

'Ah.' Ginny half-smiled at the last remark but replied seriously. 'Dad was in the army before I was born.' She rose and began to busy herself with minor adjustments to Lucy's reins. 'I remember nothing about that. He left the army just before I came on the scene, went into practice in Berkshire, dropped the ''Martyn'' from his surname and we never moved from the house where I was born.'

'And what were they like, your parents?'

'Well…' How strange to be talking of her father to this man, and yet it was less fraught than she might have feared. 'Dad was a quiet man in a way, a bit older than Mum but with a brilliant sense of humour. We laughed a lot. He could find something amusing in most circumstances. And Mother…'

Remembering, her lips curved. 'The very first thing you'd have noticed was that she was so very attractive. And bright. And popular, but also…' She was expressing an idea which had lingered vaguely at the back of her mind for a long time. 'Also unfulfilled, I suppose you would say. She would never have said so, but I think she regretted not having gone to university, or art college, perhaps.'

Suddenly she remembered the picture that she'd given to Hugo last night, and decided that avenue was best avoided. 'She married young and missed out on having a career. Life was different in those days.' She sighed reminiscently. 'As far back as I can remember she was determined I should do something with my life.'

'Well.' Jake studied her averted profile. 'In that respect she must have been pretty happy with the outcome.'

'Yes, she was.' Ginny's smile won over her sorrow. 'She and Dad were pleased as punch—even more so when I started with such an old company in London.'

'And marriage? Did she never long for you to meet a suitable young man, settle down with him and start a family?'

'If she did—' her tone was slightly sharp '—she kept it very much to herself.' How could this man know how much anguish he was causing? Standing there looking at him, knowing how she felt, conscious that her first and only duty was to hide those feelings, she knew she must not allow this conversation to continue. 'Shall we go on?'

'If that is what you want.' Lazily he got to his feet and stretched. 'For myself, I am perfectly content to stay here for the rest of the afternoon, but we can head back via the lake. With luck we might be in time to see some ducks coming in. Now...' He took a step closer. 'If you want a hand up...'

But Ginny was disturbed by the very image of placing her foot in his cupped hands, by the thought of the easy power which would lift her up and into the saddle. So disturbed that she didn't wait, just put her foot into the stirrup and swung herself up, and spent

a moment fussing with the reins before she judged
herself calm enough to look at him.

She found him standing there, hands on hips, eye-
brows raised in mild amusement. Turning away, he
casually tossed the word 'Chicken' over his shoulder,
and it seemed so very apt that vexed colour flooded
into her cheeks, making her glad he was no longer
looking in her direction.

When they at last got back to the house, the sun
was dropping down beneath the horizon and she dis-
mounted at the house while Jake led Lucy back to the
stables. It was a relief to have a quick swim followed
by a leisurely hot shower, with all the time she needed
to lavish on hair and skin.

Then, dressed in a simple skirt and blouse, she went
down to the kitchen where she set about making tea.
Inside she was surging with all kinds of rampant emotions, feelings she would not admit had anything to
do with the knowledge that she and Jake were alone
in the house. And yet the very fact that Martha, the
housekeeper, was taking a few days' holiday was right
at the forefront of her mind—reason enough for nervous dismay as well as rising excitement.

Reflecting on this contradictory state of mind, she
poured herself some tea, and was just reaching for a
second cup when Jake strode into the kitchen.

'I'm taking you out to dinner tonight.' His back
was to her as he scrubbed his hands, and then he
swung round and paused, his attention caught by her
unguarded expression. 'I thought you might like to go
to the country club.'

'Oh.' It was ridiculous to feel even a twinge of

disappointment, but she had been so busy planning, looking forward to an entire evening alone… And yet, how much more sensible to avoid the temptations of such an intimate situation. 'I hope you don't feel you have to lay on an outing for me. In fact, if you'd prefer to go on your own…'

The violet eyes were very intense and searching. 'Is that what you really think, Ginny?'

'I…' Her skin grew warm. 'I would hate to think I was being a nuisance.'

'For God's sake.' Reaching out for the biscuit tin he wrenched off the lid with barely controlled anger. 'Do you work at being obtuse? Can't you get the message? I like having you here. Repeat, *I* don't actually find you a nuisance. At least, not *that* much of one.'

'I'm sorry.' She wanted to soothe him. 'Tell me, what does one wear to go to the country club? I didn't come prepared for a series of sophisticated outings.' With relief she saw him relax.

'Oh…casual more than sophisticated.' He was standing in the doorway, long legs crossed at the ankle, drinking tea and looking at Ginny who was now sitting, gently rocking, in one of the chairs by the fireside. 'And I would think whatever you wear you'll outshine every other woman there by a factor of ten.'

There was a moment of leaping, searing pleasure when she allowed her mind to float free before struggling to bring things back into perspective. 'Jake!' The reprimand was designed to repress her own joy *and* trepidation. For if he was to speak like this, behave like this, even without touching her, for heaven's sake, what hope was there? 'It will have to be the same skirt I wore in New York.'

'That old thing.' He sighed provocatively and grinned. 'Well, if you must…'

And later on, slipping it over her head, she smiled to herself, made up her mind to keep things cool, to enjoy herself and make the most of the occasion. So long as she maintained a sensible degree of control there was no reason whatsoever why they shouldn't have a perfectly pleasant evening.

Riffling through the hangers in her wardrobe was not an exhausting task, but she wished she had something other than the white blouse—but then she saw her favourite black stretchy silk top. How could she have forgotten? Eagerly her hands reached out for it.

And it was perfect. True, it showed a vast amount of honey-coloured skin, a generous curve of breast, but it was demure in a subtle way, with long tight sleeves. And so elegant. She rummaged in her small jewellery box and found a velvet choker with her grandma's gorgeous brooch… A tear stung unexpectedly at her eyes. Except that she hadn't been her grandmother, any more than Tom had been her father…

Damn. Impatiently she blinked and decided to redo her hair, using some combs to twist it into a casual knot on top of her head.

There! Her reflection pleased her. This was more stylish. It made her neck seem longer and showed off the dangling earrings to match the choker. High heels tonight, rather than boots, and she was ready. Face lightly made-up, eyelashes a mite longer and darker than usual, lips just touched with a soft pink... She didn't dare keep Jake waiting a moment longer.

Down the long curving staircase she walked, head high, fingers lightly skimming the balustrade. There was no doubt about it—looking good was synonymous with feeling good. Then Jake stepped from the shadows and stood there, watching. It made her hesitate, aware of the blood pounding in her veins, before she calmed herself again and reached the hall.

Jake came forward then, stood looking for so long that she could feel temptation, sweet and dangerous, flooding through her. He took her hand and raised it to his mouth. 'By a factor of twenty.' His voice was slightly ragged. He turned and led her to the door.

Afterwards, Ginny wondered how she had ever reached it, for she could have sworn her legs were incapable of supporting her.

CHAPTER SIX

A BALMY night, an open roadster, a tape of the most insidiously romantic music, a devastatingly handsome man at the wheel—what more could a girl ask for? she asked herself with a desperate determination to mock. Nothing, was the daunting reply to the cynical query. There was nothing more in the world she would ask for, and if she were fated, like the *Flying Dutchman*, to travel like this through all eternity, then she would happily, joyfully, embrace her fate.

But all too soon they were turning from the road into a wide driveway, then pulling up beside a cluster of low buildings with Spanish-style arches, wrought-iron and tumbling bougainvillea.

Jake's touch was protective as he helped her from the car. 'I hope the wind hasn't blown your hair about.' A finger tracing across her forehead set off tiny shock waves.

'No.' Did her voice sound strangled? 'No, I'm sure it's fine.' Reaching up for a businesslike examination, her hand encountered his, and was instantly captured. He led her towards the subdued light of the foyer.

'You're right, of course.' He held open the glass door. 'You're quite perfect.' Gentle mockery was a perfect antidote for the compliment—a blessing, since she mustn't allow herself to be convinced. That would be the most stupid thing of all...

Then they were in the bar, threading their way through the amiable chattering crowd of people, several of whom exchanged greetings with Jake. She was seated at a table while he wandered off to speak with one of the waiters.

At the far side of the room she caught sight of the Colonel, distinctive in carriage and dress even with his back to them. Switching her gaze to Jake, she was just in time to see a woman detach herself from one of the groups and greet him with extreme affection. She kissed him on each cheek before, wide-eyed with wonder, she gazed up at him, both hands flat against his chest.

More of a girl than a woman, Ginny decided with a jealous pang, hardly more than twenty.

Blonde hair tumbled over gorgeous sun-tanned shoulders, rippling in waves very nearly to her waist. Her navy minidress did nothing to hide her shapely figure and long legs… They were coming across. Jake was smiling down at some remark, while she…she flashed her white teeth and the gleam in the blue eyes suggested she had just won the State lottery.

Why, Ginny asked herself with a feeling of despair, was she being so bitchy?

Seconds later Jake was murmuring introductions which were barely acknowledged on the girl's part. 'Oh… Hi.' The cursory glance told Ginny she did not rate highly—an attitude she could only admire since she hated the tearing envy she was feeling for Jake's 'friend and neighbour, Bonnie White'. Hated that sun-streaked blonde hair, those long legs. Hated the way the baby-blue eyes widened when Jake said anything even remotely amusing.

'I think your friends are going in now, Bonnie.' Oh, yes, and she hated that soft, indulgent note in Jake's voice when he spoke to this…*ingénue*.

'Oh, yes.' The child pouted, fluttered her lashes. 'But I shan't go unless… I want to see you while you're here, Jake…you promise you will call me? Promise?' She wheedled.

'I promise.' He smiled patiently. 'As soon as I can.'

'Don't forget.' There was a hint of imperiousness as she rose and began to move away. Then she tossed back, 'Oh, goodbye Miss… It's been so nice.' And she was at once absorbed into the group being shepherded in the direction of the restaurant at the same time as a waiter came and placed long glasses of icy drinks on the table in front of them.

'What a very pretty girl.' Her voice rang with insincerity even though she was speaking the simple truth.

'Yes.' His tone was dry as he followed the direction of her glance. 'Yes, she grows prettier each time I see her.'

'A neighbour, you say?' Her voice was clipped, and she refused to look at him, concentrating her attention on the comings and goings of others.

'Yes.' *His* attention was concentrated on her face; she had the odd idea that he was in some way amused. 'Her parents own the land adjoining ours.'

'I see.' Such scrutiny was making her feel foolish, slightly embarrassed and maybe even overwrought— which might have been why her next comment was

very nearly a blunder. 'I suppose all these old fami-
lies—' She had been about to say 'intermarry'. She
bit the word off. 'Are lifelong friends…allies.'

And, since it was becoming impossible to resist the
strong pull he exerted, she flicked back her lashes and
looked at him. She was immediately taken aback and
confused by his smiling expression.

'Mmm.' He composed his features. 'Yes, they are
both of those. And often, very often, they do marry
each other. Is that what you were about to ask?'

'No.' Indignation and embarrassment fought for
control. 'Why should I ask that when it's of no interest?'

'Oh.' There was sighing mockery from Jake. 'How
disappointing. I was sure you were going to say how
foolish it would be for me and Bonnie to…'

'You are being ridiculous.' But his attitude was a
relief. She felt the beginnings of a smile. 'But, since
you mention it, and if my opinion were sought, then
I should be forced to say there would seem to be
positive advantages…' A weary sigh from him was
ignored, but she couldn't resist another tiny barb—it
was a way of getting back at Bonnie. 'Besides, your
parents would be delighted.'

'You think so?' He appeared to consider her com-
ments seriously.

'Bound to be, I imagine. Isn't it what all land-
owners do? Try to match their acres with their children?'

'Mmm.' He frowned, raised his glass and drank
without taking his eyes from hers. 'Tell me, Ginny,
did your father have a partner?'

'Ye-es.' She was suspicious. 'A junior partner.'

'And did your parents ever point out the advantages of you marrying his junior partner?'

A picture of Donald Mackay flashed into her mind—short, stout and, she suspected, middle-aged before he'd reached primary school. But she repressed her desire to laugh and shook her head soberly as she prepared to perjure her way out of this absurd conversation. 'No. You see, you didn't ask if his partner was a man…or a woman.'

'Well…' His eyes sparkled as if he could see right through her deceit but was prepared to go along with the joke. 'I admit that could affect the outcome.' And then, before any more could be said on the subject, a waiter came to tell them their table was ready and they moved into the dining room.

Ginny's first impression was of discreet lighting, trees and plants in huge pots, and a rich and elegant clientele eating and talking against a background of subdued but rhythmic music. When they were shown to their table at the far end, she saw the room was entirely open to a small terrace with a parquet area where already one or two couples were moving in time to the Latin beat.

The staff were attentive and the meal delicious: spicy guacamole, barbecued seafood kebabs with salad and passion-fruit mousse for dessert.

'You must have been hungry.' Jake leaned forward to refill her glass.

'I was.' She grinned as she manoeuvred the last tiny spoonful of mousse from her dish, sighing with pleasure as she dabbed her mouth with her napkin. 'I was, and the food was quite wonderful. Thank you.'

'Perhaps you would like another of those?' He indicated the empty dessert glass.

'No,' she replied, with a shade of reluctance. 'Though I confess, I am tempted. But, no—too much might just spoil the overall effect. But…I would love to have the recipe, if that could be arranged.'

He grinned, shaking his head. 'Michel would be flattered, and would doubtless be happy to give you the recipe—minus one or two ingredients so the results would compare unfavourably with his. No, best to ask Martha. I'm sure she can make something very similar. She should be back within a week or so.'

'Jake.' Her tone was outraged. 'You know I can't possibly hang on here for that length of time.'

'Relax. Relax.' He was smiling. 'I was teasing.' His hand reached out and covered hers. The smile faded, his expression grew serious, carefully persuasive, which puzzled her until she remembered how unpredictable she had been—alternately encouraging and discouraging. 'But why don't you take my advice, make it easy for yourself and stay for a day or two?'

How she wished she could allow herself to do just that—even remembering the reason why she must not was like a blow to her heart. How she wished she could blot it all from her mind, longed for the innocence which would give her the freedom to follow her own instincts and…

'And make it easy for me.' Jake was taking her hand to his mouth. She felt his lips on the sensitive skin of her palm. 'You know it's what I want above everything.'

For a moment the blood sang in her veins. She allowed her defences to weaken, allowed herself to think of the possibilities—for, of course, to a certain extent he was right. She could, if she so decided, wait a little longer—her company was unlikely to cut up rough over a few extra days, which was all she would require.

It would be possible for her to go on enjoying his *companionship*, nothing else. She could even absorb a little more of what could so easily have been *her* native culture—it was her birthright when all was said and done.

And even if a little flirtation should creep in—she was too honest to deny that possibility completely— then she would see it was a mild, low-level affair. She had had plenty of experience of that over the years. There would be no strings, no one need be hurt, and at the end they could part with tender memories…

'Ginny…' When he spoke she realised that he was still holding her hand, that she seemed unable to find the strength to pull it away. At the same time she registered the expression in his eyes, recognised his carefully controlled desire—and the wild flare of her own responses which had to be instantly doused.

Dread rose in her like a choking gag. She had no idea how long she would be able to…

'Jake.' She smiled with an insincerity which hurt almost as much as sliding her hand from his. 'I've already said I would love to stay and, if you ask me, then I could easily be persuaded to come back when

I have more time—next year perhaps. But…right now, I must get back to work and…' The words almost stuck in her throat. 'And to my life in London.'

In that instant Jake's eyes appeared to change colour, from that wonderful clear violet to a dark and more menacing shade, full of sombre forebodings, and inducing a shudder in the region of her spine.

But relief came from an unexpected quarter—one that was more than welcome from Ginny's point of view. She looked up and saw the Colonel.

'Miss Virginia.' He gave a faint bow and turned to Jake. 'M'boy, I was wondering if your parents got off safely.'

'Ah.' Jake rose, his manners instinctive, and Ginny saw that the look of cold, bleak anger had gone. His manner was cool, calm and quite normal. 'Yes, they should be well on their way now. I expect a call in the morning before they sail.'

'I've arranged flowers for their stateroom.'

'Very kind of you, sir. Will you join us?'

'No, my boy, I shan't intrude, but—'

But just then Bonnie appeared behind Jake, her arm snaking about his waist.

'Jake, honey, remember this tune? I specially asked them to play it so I could ask you to dance with me.' Pouting delightfully, she turned her searchlight smile on Ginny. 'You will forgive me for stealing him away, Miss…?'

'Of course.' How chilly and disapproving and middle-aged she sounded—and how much more subtle to have hidden her feelings.

'Bonnie, I—' Jake began.

'Go on, my boy,' the Colonel interrupted. 'I shall be delighted to keep Miss Ginny company while you dance with this child.' And a moment later Jake was moving round the tiny dance floor to some smoochy number Ginny couldn't place, and she was only half listening to what her companion was saying.

'…a very old Virginian family—they have a huge spread next to Marion's. In fact—' he lowered his voice confidentially, his eyes twinkling, '—I believe Eugene—Bonnie's father, that is—he and Marion at one time… But then she met Hugo and that was that…'

His words percolated slowly. Refusing to focus on Jake and Bonnie, Ginny was watching the couple next but one on the dance floor, but when the Colonel's words had snapped into place she smiled cynically.

'Yes.' Her manner was forced. 'Yes, I can imagine. She met Hugo and…that was that.' About to make an excuse and go to the powder room, she was stopped by the look of frowning frustration in the Colonel's eyes.

'It's that same feeling, darn it.' He shook his head with practised charm. 'That fleeting likeness I can't place.'

'Oh.' Ginny subsided onto her seat, her smile becoming more fixed as she wondered how to deflect his interest. 'But you've known so many women, Colonel—or so I'm told! Maybe one or two of us look alike.' She kept her tone light and teasing.

'Mmm. You may be right, but… I don't think it's that, not exactly.'

'Well, as I said before, I know we have never met

before.' Determined to make her break now, she pushed back her chair. 'I'd have remembered. Now, please would you excuse me for a moment...?' And she made her escape.

In the Ladies' room she studied her reflection with a worried expression. Was there a chance, that her mother and the Colonel had met? Or had he, perhaps, seen her photograph? He might have been in Hugo's confidence. Or was he merely picking up that elusive resemblance to Hugo which she had been aware of last night?

Oh, God! It was so confusing, so worrying, and now, gazing at her reflection with concentrated intensity, she could find nothing to give a clue either way. Huge luminous eyes stared back... If the Colonel could see something, why not others?

She picked up her bag and turned away with a feeling of despair. She was examining an unremarkable print in the corridor when she saw Jake waiting in the empty foyer.

'I'm sorry about that!'

'Oh, Jake!' She affected surprise. She determined to be cool, uninvolved—if *only* he would help. 'Sorry?' She gave a tiny frown while puzzled brown eyes searched his. 'But why on earth should you apologise?'

'You know why.' And he turned her so they were facing in the same direction, his hand sliding the length of her inner arm till his fingers found hers and they linked. 'Because I would much rather have danced with you.'

'Oh, come *on*.' The tone of light reproof successfully concealed her disturbed feelings. Just the pressure of his arm on hers, the touch of his fingers, and every plan, every strategy… 'No man could ever be sorry to have danced with Bonnie,' she continued, in a spirit of self-mutilation. 'You made a very striking couple. I think everyone who saw you would agree.'

'Look.' There was now a touch of repressed fury in his voice as they came face to face with themselves in the darkened glass. 'Look, damn you. Now that is what I would call a very striking couple.'

For a long fraught moment they stood there, each glaring at the other before some of the tension seemed to ease from him and her breathing began to slow.

'And now…' His voice softened. 'Now, Miss Ginny Browne, of Brockway and Laffan in the City of London…' His lips were beginning to curve. 'Will you do me the honour of having the next dance with me?'

The last time she had tried to tango was when she'd been about seventeen, when her father, in a short-lived protest against what he called 'non-music' and 'non-dancing', had decided she ought to be educated. Several old records had been unearthed and they had spent some hilarious afternoons with Mantovani.

But dancing a tango in these circumstances, and with Jake Vanbrugh, was something different—a kind of enchantment. They moved in smooth unison to the sensuous, throbbing music. His cheek was against her hair and from time to time she felt the faint graze of his chin against her cheek. Such an inexplicable, bewilderingly exciting sensation.

When the music stopped, they stood for a moment,

hands still linked, eyes searching. Ginny heard her heart beating wildly against her ribs. And then his arm came about her waist and he was hurrying her along a path to a little gazebo, overgrown and sheltered from other guests.

There he kissed her. With one finger he tipped back her head and their mouths touched. Just that. It was slow and trembling and perfect. And it set her pulses ablaze.

'Shall…?' A trailing finger brushed a strand of hair from her forehead, violet eyes gleamed. 'Shall we go?'

She nodded. Just once. And, hands entwined, stopping every few yards to touch and to taste, they made their way slowly, purposefully, to the car.

He came round to open the door for her when they pulled up in front of the house, and she slid out and stood beside him, looking up into his face, all the strong planes of it shadowy in the moonlight. Jake touched her cheek, his fingers brushing the skin, causing ripples of emotion she had never known. Her lips parted on a sigh of invitation as old as Eve herself.

Even before his mouth took control she had lost all desire to resist, had succumbed to the sheer joy of her own feelings—his co-operation adding an intense edge to this experience.

Inside, the hall was dim and cool and quiet, the only sound the ticking of a grandfather clock in the far corner and perhaps the rapid tattoo of her own heart. She clung to him as he took her, one slow step at a time, up the curving stairway, her arms twined about his neck, her mouth seeking his—all reservations obliterated, forgotten.

'Ginny.' They had reached her bedroom—one pink-shaded lamp glowed softly in a corner, the bed, wide and inviting, dominated the room. Jake's hands cupped her face—he gazed as if he could never have enough. 'Ginny, the moment I saw you...'

'Jake...' She was beginning to understand what it must mean to be under the influence of some powerful drug. It must be like this—such unreality, such a sense of euphoria, of a wondering excitement which invaded every inch of her. Resistance was no longer part of her game plan—instead, every precocious notion, every dream she had ever had, would come into play.

'Jake.' In the meantime the pleasure in simply repeating his name was intense, and she tangled her fingers in his hair, pulling him into still closer contact, and...

'The moment I saw you...' His mouth trailed kisses the length of her cheek, spoke against the corner of her mouth. 'I wanted you—and I shall go on wanting you...'

The words should have been a warning but she was too intoxicated, too hypnotised. There was one thing she wanted—to be closer to him, without any analysis of what that meant. Simply, that this journey was leading to a goal she was at last beginning to understand.

She gave a moan, a shudder, as she slid her fingers inside his jacket. There was a moment of impatience as he shrugged the garment from his shoulders, pulled off his tie, undid his shirt. And then it was all so simple, so easy—a tiny tug at the zipper at her back and he slid the figure-hugging top to her waist, pulled it from her skirt and tossed it away.

'Look.' His voice was ragged, his touch sheer magic, but he turned her round so she was forced to see herself in the mirror. A young woman, naked to the waist but for her grandmother's choker, with hair which had been pinned up beginning to collapse about her face.

If an artist had planned an arousing picture he could scarcely have improved things. A demure yet knowing child, mouth bruised and swollen with kissing, eyes brown and limpid. And in the background the tall, powerful man—and he was touching her, expressing some of the wonder they were sharing.

Suddenly shy, she turned and laid her cheek against his chest, rubbing at the triangle of dark hair.

'Don't!' It was a laughing, tortured contradictory plea. 'Don't do that… I want to *see* you and…do you know what you're doing to me?'

She didn't. She knew only what was happening to her—rejoiced that he was part of it, that he was making her life so wonderful, that she had no wish to escape…

They were lying on the bed. She felt light, teasing kisses on her face, her eyes, her mouth. Until suddenly he grew serious, pushed her back against the pillows and spoke with powerful intensity. 'I want to make love to you for the rest of my life.'

Something reminded her—afterwards it was impossible for her to decide what. Maybe it was his absolute conviction, the implication of long-term commitment... An innocent flirtation, she had decided, no strings... And here they were, on the brink...

Terror struck. She was swept with mind-shattering speed from her pedestal. Quickly, as if doused with cold water, she crossed her arms in front of her, rolled from the bed, reaching out to a chair for her flowered satin robe. She had belted it about her waist before she could find the courage to turn and face Jake, who was still lying on the bed. And on his face, when she dared look, she saw an expression she had never expected to encounter, one which stabbed her to the soul.

'Jake.' One shaking hand went to push the fall of hair back from her forehead. 'Jake, what can I say?'

It was a long time before he spoke. Then, with an easy move he stood, looming over her with a hint of threat. 'In the circumstances I would suggest your best plan is...to say nothing. Anything you do say is liable to be misunderstood.' He reached out for his shirt, unhurriedly, while keeping his eyes fixed firmly on her face. He thrust his arms inside it, the ripple of strong shoulder muscles, the gleam of dark hair against the smooth brown skin of his chest a form of torture to her.

'On the other hand...' he continued, and she had the distinctly uneasy feeling that while she had been immersed in her thoughts he had not been unaware of the direction they were taking—something which her sudden scald of colour had doubtless confirmed... She raised a defiant chin, raised an eyebrow, inviting him to continue.

Bending, he picked up his tie from the carpet, knotted it with a few deft moves, pulled it taut, ran a finger along the inside of his collar. 'On the other hand, that might be making life rather easier for you than you deserve.'

Blankly she looked at him, struggling with the sob which was forcing its way from her throat—but not for the world would she let him know how his tone of cold animosity was wounding her, cutting her to the heart. In an effort at self-defence she turned away, inadvertently catching her reflection—which did little enough for her esteem.

Where had it all gone? she asked herself with no hope of a satisfactory answer. All that glowing excitement, the bloom and enchantment of a woman in love which had been so striking such a short time ago. 'I...' she began, with no clear idea of how she meant to continue. But any need for development was cut off by the sudden shrill of a telephone somewhere in the house, sufficiently startling for her to whirl around to face him.

For an intense, fraught moment they stared at each other, then, as the ringing continued, he turned away. His feet could be heard crossing the landing, entering another bedroom. The intrusive noise ceased, was replaced by the soft murmur of his voice and then he was back, leaning in the doorframe while she had not moved from the spot.

'I'm sorry.' His voice was taut, denying the words he had spoken. 'I must go down to the stables.' He gave a quick glance at his watch, a weary sigh. 'I shouldn't be long. We have to talk.'

From downstairs the sound of a closing door told

her he had gone. Distantly she heard an engine fire and still she stood as if in a dream. But at last a little life returned. She moved to the dressing-table and sat, slowly began to remove the earrings, her choker, pulled the pins from her hair, seeing the collapse of the rich tresses as deeply symbolic. Difficult to identify this woman—faded, lacklustre—with the one who had been reflected such a short time before. Now, with all hope, all animation wiped away, she was very nearly plain.

There was just one thought in her mind—the one that had been hammering so relentlessly for attention for the past few days, the one she had chosen to ignore, knowing full well she was playing with fire. Now she was badly burnt, and her only hope of recovery was to do now what she ought to have done before. She had to get away, back to London, where she could bury herself in her work and perhaps, eventually, be able to wipe this mad episode from her mind.

At last, exhausted, she reached for her nightdress, pulled it over her head, switched off the lights and buried her face in the pillows. The tears came then. The misery which she had been trying to stem for so long could be held back no longer. There was a certain relief in allowing it to overwhelm her.

The weeping had run its course but she was still light years from sleep when she heard Jake return. In her imaginative state she found something heart-rending about his step in the hall—but that was sheer foolishness, more to do with her own emotions than those he was likely to have.

Then, before she knew it, he was opening her door. She held her breath as he spoke her name once, twice. She was surprised that the noise of her heart hammering against her ribs was not a betrayal. But, no, again he spoke her name, this time more of a whisper, a weary sigh. Then, just as she knew she could keep up this cheap pretence no longer, the door closed gently.

She breathed again, lay there in the dark, wide-eyed and tragic. Wishing with all the futile strength of her being that she had allowed the past to keep its secrets.

CHAPTER SEVEN

BEFORE Ginny could find the courage to go downstairs next morning she packed her case. It wasn't so
much that she was making a statement of intention,
rather, it was a calming exercise. An attempt, only
partly successful, to reduce the emotional pressure after last night's miscalculations.

What on earth, she asked herself incredulously, had
made her imagine she could control things between
her and Jake? When she had known from that very
first moment... Love at first sight was such a cliché,
not the kind of thing you expected to happen—certainly not at the age of twenty-six, when you thought
you were well past the danger age for flights of fancy.
When you thought you had your life mapped out—
first the career then, perhaps, if a suitable man turned
up...

The ache was back in her chest. But it seemed she
had been dealt the cruellest hand fate could find for
her... Oh, God, if she started on that again she would
never be able to face him, and, as it was, after a sleep-
less night she felt jaded. It was a depressing idea
which her mirror was only too ready to confirm.

Brushing aside a tear, she surveyed her reflection
critically. She wore the same trousers that she'd worn
that first day in New York. The outfit which had
pleased her then now looked mundane, a touch dreary.

Or was it, perhaps, a mistake to blame the clothes? She was so pale underneath the golden tan which she'd gained over the last few days. All the colour, all the vitality seemed to have drained from her face...

What was the use of so much self-torture? She had no choice but to go downstairs, to drink coffee, to eat breakfast, and the sooner she did so the sooner the ordeal would be over... She gave a gesture of defiance as she touched her mouth with a little more lipstick, tested out a wan, unconvincing smile, and ran downstairs before her determination could leach away.

In the act of pouring coffee, Jake turned when the door opened and directed a searing glance at her which appeared to draw all kinds of conclusions from her features. Ginny looked about her in trepidation, almost hoping to encounter Martha's friendly smile, but she knew they were alone—which was a great pity.

'Good morning.' Nothing could be gauged from his tone, which was detached, expressionless.

'Jake.' She was diffident, self-conscious—rather than clear and positive as she had aimed to be. 'Good morning.'

'Coffee?' He held the pot poised over a cup.

'Thank you.' As he poured she took her seat at the table, shook out her napkin, and as he sat down she looked at him. 'Jake... I...' She bit her lip.

A raised eyebrow, a cool, enquiring look did nothing for her tensions, and she forced herself to continue. 'Jake...what time did you get back last night? I'm awfully sorry, I must have fallen asleep.'

'Well…' He drank from his cup and replaced it on the saucer. 'I wasn't *awfully* late.' His mocking of that particular word normally would have made her grin— now it was an irritant, exactly as he'd intended it to be. 'I did come into your bedroom, but there was no reply.'

'Well, as I said…' She hated lying, especially to him, but since their whole relationship was based on deceit, did it matter? 'I'm sorry.'

With great care she took some butter and spooned a little preserve onto the plate beside the toast. 'Jake—' the word burst out without thought '—I am sorry about what happened. Things got out of control, and as I told you…I'm not into multiple relationships.' Deceit was becoming increasingly simple. 'I'm…I'm not…'

His tone was harsh. 'Are you implying now that you are not free?' He regarded her with considered contempt. 'And you are so involved with this man that within a day or two of leaving him you are very nearly in bed with someone else?' He seemed to find her rising colour of some significance. 'Not what I would call a very serious commitment. Scarcely the romance of the century.'

'Is that…' Tears were stinging behind her eyes and her voice was not entirely steady, but she raised her chin defiantly. 'Is that what you really think of me?'

He rubbed a weary hand between his eyes. 'What am I supposed to think? Oh…' He gave an impatient shake of his head, rose and paced across the room. 'No.' He sighed deeply. 'I'm the one who is sorry. I should not have said what I did. I had no right and it was…'

'You were provoked…'

'It's probably good for my ego.' He gave a slightly bitter laugh. 'Anyway, forget it. I certainly have.'

'Oh…' That last comment shocked her—that he could so carelessly dismiss what had been for her the most profound, the most searing… But of course, unlike her, he was most likely enjoying such affairs every other night…

The thought made her long to howl with self-pity. She swallowed a morsel of toast, rather surprised that it didn't quite choke her, and sipped some coffee. Then, making a decision, she straightened her spine and spoke in the same casual tone he had used. 'But you don't seem… How can I put this? You seem…unhappy…disillusioned. Angry with me, despite what…'

'All of that except the last.'

'Jake?' She was puzzled, and frowned.

'Randy had to be put down last night.'

His words hung in the air—the stark pain hit her like a kick in the stomach and she longed, with all her strength, to go and put her arms round him, to give him comfort. But that was exactly what she dared not do, and words were so utterly banal.

'Jake… I'm so…so sorry.'

'That was the telephone call…' He swung round from where he was standing at the window and smiled bleakly. 'The call which came so opportunely.' He spoke through his teeth. 'It was from Miguel to say he had had to call the vet. He had been trying to

contact me but we must have been at the club…
Randy was in great pain and I had to give permission
for them to…to do what was necessary.'

When they'd been at the club. Her mind was almost
blank with the misery of it. If it hadn't been for her
visit, this visit, which she ought never to have made,
he would most likely have been at home, and then…

'Your parents will be devas—'

'Oh—they rang half an hour ago; they send their
love. Should be about to sail now…'

'Did you tell them? About Randy, I mean?'

'No. There was no point in spoiling their cruise
and— Damn!'

He glared at the jangling telephone, snatched the
receiver impatiently from the wall and uttered a weary
sigh as he listened to what was being said. All of
which gave Ginny the chance simply to look at him
under the pretence of finishing her coffee.

There was no earthly reason why she should deny
herself that pleasure, when very soon… She stared at
the dark grey trousers, cut low on the hips—the kind
of immaculately tailored casual wear which appealed
to her. Dark blue shirt, silk tie—all very smart and
impeccable… Clearly it had not been his intention to
spend the day in country pursuits…

She sighed, rose and began to collect the things
from the table onto a tray, starting to tune into his
conversation as it was coming to an end. It was all to
do with business—a problem of some importance
which was forcing him to make decisions.

'Yes, get on to Carrington right away. We don't
want any misunderstandings on this one. After that,

try Geoff Hoare. You might have to contact him at home. I seem to think he's not fully recovered... No! No, I don't want my father to be involved; it's one of those things which will sort itself out, but if he did hear I wouldn't put it past him to fly back from... No, not a word... I shall be with you just as soon as I can... Mmm... Well, within the next few hours, I would say... Yes. Goodbye, Karen. See you soon.'

Turning round abruptly, Jake caught Ginny's eye—he could hardly fail to notice her intense interest, but not, she hoped, the pang of jealousy she had felt when she understood he had been speaking with his secretary. Nevertheless, his raised eyebrow brought a wave of colour rushing into her cheeks which no amount of self-discipline could control.

'I'm sorry, Ginny.' A couple of steps brought him close. Her lungs filled with the faint but distinctive scent of his cologne and she could have sworn she felt the heat from his body, but most likely she was mistaken. She gazed up.

'Sorry?' The word was repeated blankly.

'I have to go back to the city.'

'Oh?' Relief ought to have been her reaction, so why this sudden feeling of desolation? 'Oh, I see.' Making an effort, she half turned, picking up the tray. 'Well...' She gave a tiny forced laugh and walked towards the kitchen. She paused, balancing the tray on one hip as she hesitated by the open door. 'As it happens I had my mind made up. I must make a move today.'

The intensity of his expression caused her to catch her breath but her averted head would surely hide her pain. She put down her tray and began to stack the crockery in the dishwasher.

'Leave that, for heaven's sake.' His tone was impatient, peremptory.

'I don't want to leave a mess for Martha when she comes back.' How prim and self-righteous she sounded!

'There won't be. There's a whole army of women who come in to help.'

'That didn't take a minute.' She rinsed her hands and dried them while looking out at the sweep of parkland—the majestic trees, the horses grazing contentedly in the adjoining field. There was an ache in her chest as she admitted she was seeing it for the last time. She would never dare to come back...

As she turned she fixed on an artificial smile, dazzling and contrived. 'May I beg a lift from you?'

'You need not beg. You simply have to ask.' His eyes searched her features with a desperate probing, as though seeking an answer to an insoluble problem. 'And of course you may...'

Never had she seen him so sombre. Of course, it was all to do with Randy—she need not make any connection with it having anything to do with Ginny Browne. But she longed, with all her heart and soul, to put her arms about him, to comfort him in the tender way a woman could soothe a man. Not with sex—although that was a powerful component—this was not the time for sex. It was simply the time to take a step forward, to pull his head down to hers and to murmur all the kind, emollient words which might help to ease the pain he was feeling...

But of course she had already decided that that was denied her—along with the opportunity to do all the ordinary little things women did for the men they loved... She bit her lip, turned away and spoke over her shoulder with a tiny catch in her voice which he must have picked up. 'What...what time do we leave?'

'As soon as we can. I'll get Neil to fly us. He's our pilot, when we need one. I'll give him a ring while you go and pack.'

'I've already done that.' The words were out before she could consider.

'I see.' It was an endless moment that they stood gazing at each other—she wishing she had cut off her tongue rather than reveal her plans, and he clearly drawing all kinds of conclusions, though she doubted any of them would come close to the truth. Certainly the truth that she dared not trust herself in his company was not one which would occur to him.

In no time at all they were sitting together in the executive jet as it headed north across the Delaware *en route* for New York. There was a sense of relief that she had found the strength to stick to her decision, but it was impossible to pretend there was no grief as they skimmed over the Vanbrugh ranch and made a sweep over the house. Her forehead pressed on the window to catch the last elusive glimpse.

Perhaps there was a chance, just a chance, that she and Hugo might meet up some time in the future. It was a decision he would have to make. But any such meeting would be on neutral ground, most likely in London if he ever came to the UK on business.

Jake, it appeared, had lost interest in the sheaf of papers he had been frowning over. There was a reluctant pleasure in being obliged to turn towards him as he spoke. 'You did say you might like to come back next year.'

'Yes, I did, didn't I?' Ginny's slightly caustic tone caused his manner to change from the comparatively benign to one more guarded. They stared at each other for a moment before he went on, slowly.

'Am I to conclude, then, that you have changed your mind about that?'

'Jake.' Suddenly her eyes ached with tears—that damned rock was firmly back in the middle of her chest and... She surprised herself by reaching out a hand to cover his. 'Jake, it's got to be the best thing. Surely you can see...?'

'If you're telling me the truth, I...'

'What?' All her suppressed nerviness erupted before she could check it. Then she continued more moderately, 'What on earth do you mean?'

'Simply what you said last night.' The narrowed eyes surely signified suspicion. 'I—and I'm sure most people would agree—find it hard to reconcile what happened between us with any very serious relationship you might...'

Anger and misery made her sound much more abrasive than she intended. 'But even if we try to achieve perfection, we are not always successful. Any student of human nature would confirm as much.' And if you don't believe me then ask your father for his opinion, she added cattily, but silently.

'Mmm.' He studied her averted profile. 'I shan't argue with that, just…'

'Yes?' she challenged nervily, turning to glare.

'Just, I have this feeling—one or two things don't add up.'

'You mustn't…' With a supreme effort she tried to unwind. It would be fatal if her manner encouraged him to become too inquisitive, too questioning. 'When you don't get your own way, you mustn't turn that into a mystery.'

'If you say so.' Though he spoke lightly, she had the feeling he was unconvinced. He continued to look at her with that speculative expression. Then, as if he had come to a decision, his face cleared and his lips curved into a rather reluctant smile which caused a responsive throb deep in her stomach. 'Well, tell me, what are your plans for when you reach New York?'

'Oh…' To catch the first flight for Heathrow, was her most obvious choice. But she shrugged, pursed her lips. 'Look around for a bit. I've seen hardly anything so far. To book into my hotel again is the first thing, I suppose.'

He smiled, took her hand and squeezed it, 'That is out. You'll stay in my flat. There's masses of room.'

'Oh, no, Jake.' The very idea was lethal. It would have been easy to detach her hand—easy and sensible—but…she didn't want to. She wanted to stay like this for as long as possible and that in itself said it all.

'Thank you for the offer—I do appreciate it. But

with my plans so—so fluid it would be best if I were in a hotel and—'

'Nonsense. If you're worried about the proprieties, you needn't be. And if you're concerned about what happened...'

'Jake!' She refused to allow him to say anything about the previous night—not with her still feeling so raw, so ready to burst into tears at the least provocation. 'I prefer to be a free agent, Jake. I'll find a hotel. In fact...' She reluctantly freed her hand so she could look in her handbag. 'I have the Excelsior's number right here...'

'You could stay in the penthouse in the Vanbrugh building—Mother and Father wouldn't mind.'

'Jake, please. Will you allow me to run my own life?'

'Okay.' He shrugged. 'Okay, if that's what you want.' He sighed. 'I can see you're one very determined female lawyer.'

Her disapproving expression made him laugh and after a moment she joined in.

'But at least, when we get in, use the office. If the Excelsior is full then Karen has a list you can use.'

She nodded. It was impossible to disagree with such an eminently sensible suggestion.

Except that when she did reach the office, and Jake's attention was immediately grabbed by people from half a dozen departments, it soon became clear that almost every hotel in the immediate vicinity was fully booked—and Karen was soon obviously wearying of the whole exercise of trying.

'They too are completely booked up, Miss

Browne.' She put down the phone after trying yet another. 'Do you want me to keep on trying?'

'What is it, Karen?' Jake, at that very moment rushing through the office, paused by his secretary's desk.

'This big conference, Jake. It seems all the decent hotels are full—unless Miss Browne is willing to move further out?'

'This is ridiculous, Ginny.' He sounded mildly irritated. 'Give in and go upstairs. Karen has a key and she'll show you the apartment—that ought to clinch the deal.' He grinned, as if to demonstrate that he always got his way in the end.

Which was all too true.

The apartment was the last word in elegance—it would have taken a gold medallist in self-denial to turn down the opportunity of even a brief spell there. Besides, she was a bit unhappy with herself—conscience-stricken about her rather ungracious reaction when he had first offered her the use of the apartment. Accepting it now would ease that feeling.

The next few hours were sheer bliss as she wandered about, picking up the vibrant atmosphere of the streets, drifting into world-famous stores—so glossy and gleaming and lavish they took one's breath away. She bought a few things—gifts for friends and colleagues—and was amused when, emerging from one of the most prestigious stores, she found herself next to a tiny, scruffy box of a place offering: THE ALL-AMERICAN BACK RUB $10. Walking on, she smiled to herself, toying with various weird ideas of what that might imply.

Gathering herself together, she went on more pur-

posefully, passing a Madison Avenue pavement café
which she'd heard was famous for so-called 'babe-
watching'! She was aware as she approached that one
handsome fair man was studying her closely over the
top of his dark glasses, but he smiled philosophically
when she refused to take advantage of his implicit
invitation.

There was just so much to see—she would not have
believed it. Her mind was a blur of images and impressions: so much wealth, such high fashion, and
every other woman, or so it seemed, leading a spoiled,
pampered Pekinese dog to indicate that she had everything else.

Yes, fabulous, *fabulous* New York. But now her
legs and feet were aching, and it seemed a good idea
to head back to the apartment and plan a day of more
organised sight-seeing for tomorrow. It was so easy
to get a cab—she merely stood on the edge of the
pavement, held up her hand and one pulled up. She
climbed in and sat back in the seat, her mind fixed
upon the pleasures of the most sybaritic marble bath-
tub she had ever seen.

It was while she was lying amidst deliciously scented
bubbles that the telephone shrilled alarmingly, right
against her ear. It was easily traced to a little recessed
cupboard in the tiled wall by the bath.

'Hello?' The sound of her voice made Ginny giggle—it was husky and provocative, like a glamorous
film star's.

'Ginny.' For some reason that particular voice was

a shock, an intrusion into very intimate circumstances. Modestly she slipped a few inches lower in the water.

'J-Jake.'

'What are you doing? Have I caught you at an inconvenient moment?'

'Of *course* not,' she denied, too quickly, rather pleased he could neither see her blush nor hear her heart thumping. Then a thought flew into her mind which almost produced another giggling fit. Perhaps she should quote Marilyn Monroe: 'I just caught my big toe in the faucet and could use a plumber!' It seemed an appropriate line but she didn't use it. Her voice continued as coolly as she could have hoped. 'No, not at all. Have you solved your problem?'

'The major one.' He laughed briefly. 'But there are always others. About tonight, Ginny…'

'Tonight?' Immediately defensive, she sat up. Tonight she planned to eat the pizza she had bought and drink some coffee—if she could work out how to do that in the space-age kitchen.

'I'm going to be late. Shan't be able to pick you up till about nine-thirty, I'm afraid. But there's a pleasant little bistro close by and—'

'Jake, there's absolutely no need…'

'I *know* that.' His tone was mild. 'But it's what I want. And I hope it's something you want too. So…nine-thirty? Okay?'

'Thank you, Jake. Nine-thirty.' She replaced the receiver and subsided in the warm water with her eyes closed. She lay quite, quite still—but with her brain racing in wild overdrive.

*   *   *

In fact, it was just before nine-thirty when Jake Vanbrugh let himself into the apartment, stood for a moment in the spacious hallway and called her name as he walked into the sitting room.

He looked handsome and relaxed, and, if Ginny had been there, she would have noticed that he had found time in his hectic day to have his hair trimmed, that he was freshly shaved and smelled of that subtle distinctive cologne. She would have approved the easy style of his casual jacket, the maroon open-necked shirt, would even have noticed the fine calf shoes, but…

But Ginny was no longer in the apartment. At that precise moment she was in the queue at the airport, awaiting the security check before boarding her plane for Heathrow. And each time someone brushed against her, her eyes widened in guilty anxiety.

Again Jake called her name, frowned. As he was about to walk through to the bedrooms his eye was caught by a thick cream envelope propped up against a flower vase. It was addressed to him. His face hardened as he slipped a finger beneath the flap and extracted a single sheet of paper. Quickly he skimmed the few lines of small, neat writing.

Jake, dear,

    I made one brief call to London. I hope you don't mind. A very urgent matter is awaiting my attention so I think it is time to go. Maybe it is best this way—I hate goodbyes, don't you? Thank you for everything.

Ginny.

Stony-faced, Jake crossed to where the telephone sat on top of an antique cabinet and bent to open a door. A few buttons operated the electronic recording system which monitored all incoming and outgoing calls and he straightened up slowly as tapes whirred and connections clicked.

His expression was grim as he heard Ginny begin her pleading negotiations with an airline official and he switched it off in disgust when he faced the reality of her lying.

Teeth clenched, unseeing, he strode across to the wide picture window with its panoramic view of a thousand glinting windows. Then he turned, crumpled up the letter which he still held and hurled it from him. His fist beat several times against his forehead and he groaned. She had lied to him.

CHAPTER EIGHT

BACK in London, Ginny's time in the States began to take on the illusory aura of a dream. Once or twice in the night she woke to find her face and pillow wet. But that, and the weight of misery inside, were the only reminders that there was nothing imaginary about what had happened.

It was a blessing that Jake had left her in peace, that he had made no attempt to follow her.

Strap-hanging on the tube one day, on her way back to the Wimbledon flat which she shared with her friend Kate, she refused to acknowledge her half-formed hope that he would do just that. If his feelings had been half as strong as hers, then there was no way he could have resisted. But, as she kept telling herself so consistently, he had recognised that she meant what she had said and had acted accordingly.

The volume of work which had enveloped her on her return had been another plus. It had left her with little time to mope, to dwell on what might have been. With difficulty she suppressed a yawn, straightened up and began to edge towards the doors as the train slowed for her station. In fact, she admitted, she was tired out—emotionally and physically exhausted.

Her heels struck sharply against the pavement as she hurried the short distance to her flat. What wouldn't she give for the chance to avoid this evening's theatre trip? It had been arranged as a treat by Kate's brother Nick, who was staying with them temporarily. He had been so triumphant at acquiring three tickets for the most popular show in the West End... Ah, well. She had promised and must try to endure it, but she was not in the mood for the trite romantic lyrics, nor for sentimental music...

When she pushed open the door of the flat, Nick was heading towards the sitting room carrying a tray of mugs and a teapot. 'Here you are, sweetie. I saw you crossing the street and thought you needed reviving.'

'Thanks, Nick.' She followed him in, discarding her jacket and stepping out of her shoes with a sigh. 'I truly need this.' She subsided onto the settee and sipped thirstily.

'Busy day?'

'Frantic. In fact, after I drink this I think I'll have just half an hour on my bed—try to put the brain into neutral.'

'You work too hard, darling.' Nick was an actor—usually resting, but with all the affectations of a Henry Irving. 'That's what I was telling Kate...'

'Oh, when will she be back?'

'I was about to say, she rang and wants us to meet her at the theatre. Something to do with Colin asking her to meet a client. Bosses!' He shook a disapproving head. 'Glad I don't have one.'

'Don't tempt fate. Not when you're hoping to get a part soon.'

'No, you're right, of course. Anyway, if it's all right with you, I think I'll have a shower.'

'Fine.'

'Bless you, darling. I'll be as quick as I can.'

Ginny smiled ruefully as she closed the door of her bedroom, stripped off her black skirt and blouse and lay down on the bed with a sigh of sheer relief.

Fond as she was of Nick, she hoped his stay would not be unduly prolonged—it wasn't always convenient having the sitting room used as a bedroom... But a night or two was all right, and she didn't want to have to mention it to Kate.

Kate, of course, worried about her young, slightly irresponsible brother; who wouldn't? But he did have his own place in Brighton, and his excuse of seeing his agent about a TV role... Well, you could use that only so often... Her eyes drifted closed as drowsiness overtook her. Thoughts about Nick were submerged, and...

For a second or two she could not understand the intrusion. Then the doorbell shrilled again, urgent and imperious.

Damn you, Kate! Still sleepy, she sprang from her bed at the same time reaching out for her bathrobe. Crossing the hall, she could hear the sounds of running water from the direction of the bathroom. She threw the front door wide, her mouth forming words for her flatmate to the effect that they were supposed to be meeting up in the theatre foyer.

Only...it wasn't a woman standing there. Jake Vanbrugh was looking down at her, totally masculine, dominant as ever, and... The hallway began slowly to spin, her heart was hammering loudly against her ribcage, her mouth was dry, her hands were slippery with

perspiration. But they clung tenaciously to the heavy
door. She had no wish to repeat that stupid episode
from his New York office.

'I...' One hand made an attempt to pull together
the edges of her robe and one of her first coherent
thoughts was regret that he was seeing her in such a
state.

'Ginny.' His voice, too, had a sensual throb, a faint
hesitancy. But no, he wasn't that kind of man... 'May
I come in?'

'Of course you may.' She found her voice again,
wondered if it sounded genuinely welcoming. 'This is
a great surprise, Jake.'

'I suppose it must be,' he agreed drily, pushing the
door behind him. He stood looking at her—the striking eyes held an expression she found impossible to
identify.

'Wh—when did you arrive?' Being disorientated,
it did not occur to her to invite him into the sitting
room. All her skills as a hostess had simply evaporated. Besides, she was anxious about the sounds from
the bathroom, of water escaping down the plughole.
She could tell that Jake was diverted too, saw him
cast a quick glance towards the door before replying.

'I've just arrived. I came straight on here from the
airport.'

'How...?' But perhaps she ought not to ask this
question—it did draw attention to her discourtesy in
not leaving her address. But then he must know that
that decision had been quite deliberate. 'How did you
know where to find me?'

'It wasn't difficult.' His cool expression brought

some colour to her cheeks. 'I had my attorney call your company, and...' A shrug completed the explanation.

No one, she thought mutinously, had the right to divulge her private details. The protest sprang to her lips but remained unvoiced—after all, she knew enough to understand how easy it could be: Her telephone number was listed, for one thing, and...

She tried a negligent smile. 'Well...' She tried to plan what to do with him—Nick might just blunder into the sitting room, her bedroom was out, for obvious reasons, and the kitchen...not exactly the perfect setting for whatever was going to happen...

But, even as her mind raced in circles, the door opened and Nick emerged from the bathroom, doubly draped in towels—one wrapped round his waist, another tented about his head.

'Bath's free, Ginny!' He seemed to be directing the information towards her bedroom door. 'If you want someone to scrub your back, just call, darling.' With that he disappeared into Kate's room, where his clothes were stored, almost immediately poking his head round the door and into the hallway.

'Sorry.' He wore his disarming 'juvenile lead' smile. 'Sorry. I had no idea we had a visitor. Forgive me for interrupting.' Then he disappeared behind the closed door, leaving a silence which was very nearly tangible.

When at last he spoke Jake's manner was more grim than she had ever known it, striking at her heart like a dagger. 'It looks rather as if I'm the one who is interrupting.'

'No.' Such a half-hearted denial! Probably because of the ambivalence of her reactions. On the one hand Nick's intervention might have been timely, but on the other... In any event, Nick might just have convinced Jake that things were exactly as she had suggested in Virginia.

It was simply that she could almost read his mind, could tell how it was working and, in spite of everything, she resented his acceptance that Nick Willis could possibly be the man in her life. Nothing about him had ever appealed to her in that way, and...

All at once she remembered her manners. 'Jake, do come in.' She waved her hand in a vague gesture. 'You must have some tea.'

From the direction of the bedroom came sounds of Nick moving about, whistling, off-key, one of the tunes they might expect to hear later in the evening.

'No. No, thank you, Ginny. I simply came by to ask if you would have dinner with me tonight.'

'Oh, Jake, I'm so sorry. I don't think—'

'Ginny, darling,' the voice came as though from off-stage. A fair head and a puckish face poked round the door. 'I don't suppose you've found my blue tie? No?' From her expression he drew his own conclusions, 'I guess not. But...if we're not going to miss the first act...'

Jake's lips barely moved as he spoke. 'I can see I've come at a bad time.'

'No. It's simply...' She could have howled with misery, with frustration, with her sense of aching loss, with anger at Nick for butting in, with Jake... Oh, yes. High-degree anger with Jake, for drawing so many wrong conclusions. Surely he could see…? But men were so obtuse… Tears of self-pity were rapidly blinked away. 'Nick is taking me to a show.'

Nick, who had gone in search of the missing tie, reappeared and held it out towards Ginny. 'Can you fix this for me, love?' His sheepish grin in Jake's direction was not even acknowledged. 'I'm useless with these things.'

Ginny found it impossible to go on ignoring the niceties. 'Jake, this is Nick.' Dealing efficiently with the tie, she resisted the inclination to pull it tight. 'Nick, Jake Vanbrugh.'

'You're American.' As Nick spoke he looked at himself in the hall mirror and smiled in satisfaction. 'This girl is a whizz with ties. I've always wanted to go to the States.'

'Really?'

'Yes. And I'll make it one of these days.' Ostentatiously he glanced at his watch. 'Ginny…' he sang warningly.

'Well, I shan't hold you back.' Jake moved towards the door. 'I can see you're anxious to be off. Goodbye, Ginny.'

'Jake, I…' Desperate longing to detain him overcame her good sense. 'How long are you to be in London?'

'It's just a flying visit.' Uncompromisingly sombre, still the brilliant eyes were unable to resist searching her face. It was as if he were determined to find some explanation there.

While she, foolishly, occupied her mind with an assortment of vague regrets—that he had seen her with her hair so untidy, her face bare of even the merest touch of make-up! Oh, why hadn't she drenched herself in that heavenly duty-free perfume, instead of…? But she caught at such daft notions. If she could have chosen sensibly, wasn't this exactly the meeting she would have planned, for safety's sake?

'Well, thank you, Jake. And thank you for the invitation. Maybe next time you are in London you'll call me…'

'Yes, I'll do that.' His tone was a total contradiction of the promise. 'Goodbye, Ginny.' He looked round as Nick came in, shrugging himself into his jacket. 'Goodbye.'

'Oh, goodbye. Been nice meeting you.' The instant the door closed Nick's voice took on a new note of urgency. 'And if you don't get a move on, Ginny, we really are going to be late.'

But they made it, with a few minutes to spare, meeting up with Kate who was pacing up and down outside the theatre, rushing forward as each taxi pulled into the kerb.

'Thank heaven.' She grabbed Ginny by the arm, rushing her towards the stalls entrance. 'I was about to give you both up.' She glanced round at her brother. 'I hope you have the tickets, Nick.'

'Yes, sweetie, of course I have the tickets—and don't blame me for being late. This time I am completely innocent. It's all down to Ginny and an American who turned up on the doorstep at the last minute. I swear she was on the point of swanning off with him and standing us up.'

'Ginny?' Kate began curiously, but then they were being shown into their row amid much disturbance and the orchestra was tuning up for the overture. 'An American?' she whispered as she settled.

'Just someone I met while I was in the States.'

'You dark horse. You never mentioned...'

'Shh. It's about to begin. I'll tell you all about it tomorrow.'

And Ginny sat, hearing but not listening, applauding automatically when the others did, even sighing with pleasure at the most romantic passages—in short, giving the appearance of enjoyment when her heart and mind were elsewhere.

Next morning she was due in court, but before that she was able to squeeze in a visit to the hairdresser. It was essential to restore her morale, which had been so badly dented by the unexpected visitor.

Sitting looking at herself in the mirror, it was some relief for her to see that she didn't look quite as ghastly as she felt—in spite of a restless night. With her hair gleaming as it was now and a touch of translucent make-up much of her self-esteem was restored.

'Thanks, Charlie.' She smiled as she rose and reached for the short coat she was wearing for the first time. Her eyes encountered the stylist's admiring glance.

'Very, *very* nice,' he said, which more or less confirmed her own point of view.

'Thanks,' she said again, and before she turned away she reassured herself. Yes, the intense pink brought a glow to her skin, made her eyes look more luminous than they had looked for some time—and she just loved the contrast against her short black skirt and black silk polo. Then her heart sank. 'Heavens, I *must* rush—if you would be an angel, Charlie, and call me a taxi?'

She managed to get to court just in time, a little breathless as she walked the hundred or so yards from the office but nonetheless pleased that she had taken the time to give her damaged ego a boost.

Her case was perfectly straightforward, her preparation watertight, so her client won—always a satisfactory state of affairs. Then it was back to the office, trying to sort out in her mind what she should tackle first after lunch.

'Oh, Ginny.' The receptionist caught her as she began to climb the stairs to her room on the first floor. 'Mr Welsh said would you go to his office the moment you got back from court.'

'Oh?' After a moment's pause she continued slowly, talking over the banister. 'Did he say what it was about, Kim?'

'No.' The other girl shrugged. 'He has a client with him. Oh…hang on.' She rushed off in the direction of a persistent telephone.

As she continued thoughtfully up the stairs, Ginny frowned a little. It was unusual for the senior partner to call a junior to his office and, since she didn't flatter herself that he wanted help or advice, there was just the ghastly fear that she might have made some awful mistake…

All at once Mr Welsh's office door was thrown open and the man himself stood there, smiling with such benevolence that she knew an immediate sense of relief. It couldn't be anything too dire. 'Ah, Ginny, we saw you coming across the square, and...'

'Kim said you were anxious to speak with me.'

'Come in, Ginny, come in.' She was ushered into the opulent mahogany-lined room, which always seemed to smell of lavender polish, where the brass canopy at the old-fashioned fireplace gleamed with a hundred years of old-fashioned elbow grease. But today the view from the magnificent windows was obscured by the tall figure who turned as she stepped inside. Jake!

'Ginny.'

A note of apology in his voice, perhaps? If so it was too late. Anger flared through her—how dared he pursue her like this? He must realise...

She gave no answer to his greeting, simply allowed the firmness of her mouth and her flashing eyes to pass a message to him before she turned a more composed face to the senior partner, who was speaking again. 'I've just been hearing from Mr Vanbrugh that you and he are old friends.'

'Yes.' In a way she supposed that could be true.

'Well, he has come for some advice, Ginny, and it seems to me you're the best person to give it, since you are friends. Mr Vanbrugh is about to be married, and...'

A cloud descended on her, and she lost the thread of what her employer was saying. For some reason her mind was back at the country club where Jake had taken her, Bonnie White's face swimming clearly into view...

'So, if you'd care to take Mr Vanbrugh along to your rooms, Ginny...' She saw the two men shake hands. 'You'll find Miss Browne will be able to provide an answer to whatever problems you might have...'

And then they were walking along the corridor to her office at the front of the building—not nearly as prestigious as the one they had just left, but equally as solid and professional. She waved her client to a seat then sat herself behind the large desk.

'I like your hairdo.'

His admiring comment was unwelcome, an attempt to undermine her resolve—and doomed to failure. But in spite of herself she felt a faint smile curve her lips, and tried to conceal it by opening a drawer and rummaging for a few seconds.

When she spoke her voice hardly wobbled. She must stick to her decision to let all of this pass her by—her emotions would *not* be involved. 'Rather a surprise, seeing you this morning, Jake.'

It was difficult to look directly at him so she made a great play of straightening a pile of papers, then sat with pen poised over her notebook, making it clear that she was ready to write down whatever details were necessary.

'I thought you would have been on your way home by now.'

'No.' He spoke coolly, leaning back in the heavy leather chair. 'No, I had no intention of going back to the States until I had the chance to speak to you on your own.'

That made her raise her eyes from the desk and

stare across at him with a feeling of apprehension. If he were to mount a determined assault on her emotions then she had no idea where she would find the strength to resist. It was hard enough for her to sit here calmly, with five feet of solid wood between them, when her every instinct and longing…

'Well.' She wrenched her eyes away from his. 'I'm flattered that you have such faith in my professional skills. But I'm sure any competent lawyer… Anyway, I'd better take some notes.' And, making a start on that, she wrote his name at the top of the sheet. 'Oh, by the way—' a firm line was drawn under what she had written. 'How is Bonnie?'

'Bonnie?' For a moment he looked blank, then the blue eyes sparked with what looked very much like amusement. 'Oh, Bonnie is…very well.'

'Good. Now, if you would just explain what sort of advice you feel you need, Jake.'

'Well, the problem is…' He screwed up his face a little. Ginny had the feeling there was something slightly bogus about the situation—why should an American about to marry another American come to London in search of advice?

'My family circumstances are not exactly straightforward,' he said at last, and watched while she scribbled a few words. As she raised her head questioningly he continued. 'You see, my parents… Oh—' He broke off with a sudden recollection. 'By the way, I mustn't forget to give you their love.'

'Oh, thank you. You've heard from them, then?'

'No, but I saw them…'

'They're not home, are they?'

'No, I met them in Singapore. They're still on their trip…'

'I—I didn't know you had planned that.' Why she should know anything about his plans was difficult to explain—the way she had bailed out must surely mean she had forfeited any rights.

'It was spur of the moment rather than something planned.'

'I see. Well…' Adjusting her notepad, she frowned. 'Perhaps we'd better get on with this… You were saying about your complex family?' She threw him a faint professional smile. 'That is certainly not how it appears to outsiders, but of course it is impossible to judge without knowing all the details.'

He was watching her with a most peculiar expression, one impossible to identify but which was making her nervy and vulnerable. Hardly appropriate in someone supposed to be giving advice.

'Yes.' It was a moment before he continued. Ginny felt a relief to be required to concentrate on her job. 'My parents,' Jake went on, then stopped again for so long that she glanced up in mild exasperation. And now he spoke with such precise deliberation it was impossible for her to wrench her eyes away. 'Or rather, I *should* say, my adoptive parents…'

Whether he added anything to these words she could never afterwards have said—she was deafened by a loud noise in her head and her hand trembled so much that the pen dropped from her fingers. A large blot began to spread over the paper.

'You mean…?' Her voice was coming from a different time zone, echoing through space. She frowned with the effort of trying to assimilate such an unexpected piece of information. 'You mean Marion and…and Hugo…that they are not your natural parents?' Luminous brown eyes searched his desperately.

'That, Ginny, is exactly what I am saying.'

For an age they sat there staring at each other before he spoke again. And then in that tender, beguiling voice which had always had such a powerful effect— which from the very beginning she'd been obliged to struggle against—he continued. 'Ginny, why don't you let me—? Oh…' he grinned light-heartedly '…and I have cleared this with Mr Welsh, so excuses involving the company will be totally disregarded! Why don't you let me take you out to lunch, Ginny? I'm sure you must be hungry—I know I am. And I can tell you all about it. My trip to Singapore, I mean.'

'Yes.' She heard her voice, mild in tone, as if there had never been a wild flight from New York. No rejection of a similar invitation just the evening before. 'All right.'

And as she slipped into the pink coat in the cloakroom, taking trouble to adjust the black polo neck of her jumper and adding a smear of dark shadow to her eyelids, she wondered at such a very abject surrender.

It was all too easy to feel utterly punch-drunk at this piece of information he had so casually tossed in her direction. But she must on no account forget that before she appeared back in the office he had been confiding in Mr Welsh about details of his *marriage* plans.

Dispassionately she smeared some colour on her

lips. It was utterly pointless, this sudden feeling of euphoria, the sense of freedom she had experienced when he'd explained... And it was just as well she had not learned the two pieces of information in reverse order—then there would have been still more anguish.

No. The more she thought of it—and she was pleased to find she was thinking so rationally—the more idiotic she would be in risking further involvement. It wouldn't be too difficult to bow out, to tell Mr Welsh that a previous client required urgent help and advice. It was a moment for discretion and self-interest, a time to cut and run with even more urgency than she had shown that evening in New York.

Opening the door of the cloakroom, she found him on the landing, talking with Mr Welsh, and she could see it was not the most appropriate moment to back out. So she smiled sweetly when they were ushered off with his good wishes and an additional instruction that there was no need for her to hurry back that afternoon.

She forced herself to succumb to the possessive hand on her elbow and then, when they reached street-level, to the insidious throbbing response as his fingers slid down her inner arm and linked with hers. For the moment that touch was the only thing in the world that mattered.

CHAPTER NINE

INSTEAD of the discreet restaurant she had anticipated during the cab ride, Ginny found herself invited into a flat in one of the capital's most prestigious blocks. The kind of place where entrance was obtained by means of a plastic card and a series of punched numbers. Where a burly guard appeared behind plate glass to perform a final inspection before they were whisked skywards in the lift.

She ought not to have given in so easily. Despite an apparently cool exterior, she felt she was leaving all her common sense on the ground floor with not the least idea of how she could extricate herself without appearing unutterably gauche.

As she might have expected the apartment was, if not as spacious as the penthouse in New York, quietly luxurious and elegant, even down to the arrangements of fresh flowers in the hallway and in the sitting room.

Ginny made no attempt to conceal her cynicism. She raised her chin and summoned what she hoped was a challenging expression. 'Do you have a series of these luxury pads throughout the world?'

'Not exactly.' A level look from those startling eyes caused a tremor to rack her, made her wrench her gaze from his, searching the room rather aimlessly till she absorbed the significance of a small round table set in a window alcove. Two places were set, with a bowl of pink roses in the centre and, to one side, chilling in an ice bucket, a gold-topped bottle.

It was a relief to find such an apparent excuse for her sarcasm, but still she was unable to control the faint wobble in her voice. 'You must have felt pretty sure of me.' Her eyes glittered with easy tears, and when there was no reply she was compelled to look at him again, forcing a response.

He pushed the door behind him—closing her avenue of escape? and lay back, arms folded, eyes slightly narrowed, as if he were trying to gauge her mood. 'I was never less sure of anything in my life.'

By all the rules of an exacting training, she ought to have been able to make something of that statement, uttered in such mellow, melting tones. But the insecurity of the words was a distraction. And he added to that as he pushed himself upright with a sigh. 'At least…after last night.' He crossed the carpet towards her while she could only watch, too weak to move.

'Last…last night?' What…what had happened? She couldn't think. Not while she was looking up into the eyes which had fascinated her from the first, from which she would never be free. Aware of his hand being raised, she waited for the touch, and stopped breathing as she felt it drift gently over her hair. Realising what she was allowing to happen, she decided it was time to take control of what was happening to her.

'Jake, I…' Meaning to step away, she found instead that his hand slipped and settled at the nape of her neck, a finger moving idly against the delicate skin.

Then she heard her own voice again, this time with a note of desperation. 'Last night? Was that what you said?'

'Mmm.' A detached observer might have thought he was enjoying the situation. 'I was thinking of you and…Nick. That was his name, wasn't it?'

'You know perfectly well that was his name.'

One dark arched eyebrow made a silent comment on the sharpness of her tone. 'Well, his name, as they say, is irrelevant, but since you told me you were in some kind of relationship…'

'I didn't say that.' Then, more quietly, 'Not exactly.'

'Ah?' Clearly further elucidation was expected.

'I share my flat with a friend. Nick is Kate's brother and occasionally he inflicts himself on us for a few days.'

'Ah! But if not Nick…?' Then, after waiting for an answer which didn't come, he spoke more insistently. 'Ginny!'

Shrugging, she coloured slightly, then looked him straight in the eye, wondering as she did so why she'd ever denied herself such pleasure. She shook her head slightly, mouth curving into a smile that was close to being beatific.

'No one.' Her sense of relief was overwhelming as the full truth of the situation finally dawned on him. 'There is no one.' Luminous brown eyes gleamed with something approaching satisfaction as she made her confession. Now, at last, the truth was obvious. Now there was no reason whatever for fabricating relationships…at least not from her point of view.

'So…' She sensed he was choosing his words with great care. 'So, Nick being with you, in what could be described as suspicious circumstances, was—'

'Suspicious only if that is how your mind works.'

'Was simple coincidence,' he finished, ignoring her interruption.

'A lucky coincidence from my point of view.'

'Oh?' His hands slid from her shoulders to beneath her coat, where she felt them link about her waist. 'How so?'

'Well…' She shrugged, enjoying the sensation, revelling in the sense of power which suddenly swept over her. 'It did, after all, go some way towards confirming…what I wanted you to think.' But *why*? If only he did not ask *that* particular question. It was one which would give her great difficulty since she had not the faintest idea what he knew of her relationship with Hugo. So it was with relief that she heard him change the subject completely.

'I love this pink coat you're wearing, but…do you think you could take it off?' As he spoke he was pushing it from her shoulders.

She held out her arms to ease its passage to the floor, allowed herself to be gathered against him, felt the faintest rasp of his cheek against hers. His voice was not entirely steady. 'I've been frustrated for so long, and for so many reasons, but I'm damned if I'm going to allow a coat to come between us.'

'Jake.' It was a shaky, tremulous murmur as she turned her face, her mouth seeking his in an explosion of excitement. Frustration! As if she didn't know…

'Jake.' Her hands were tangling in his hair, lips parting on a note of lingering surrender.

Dark violet eyes blazed with something like accusation. 'I've wanted you…been crazy for you…since the first moment—the instant I set eyes on you.'

Triumph was such an ignoble reaction, but it seared through her with a power she made no effort to resist. Vaguely she recognised that her emotions were out of control; all restraints and hindrances had in some mysterious way been swept aside. There was just a tiny niggle…something about marriage plans…but that had nothing to do with her.

All she remembered was that she was free—free to love him, which she did. Free to adore him, which she did, and free, for heaven's sake, to make love with him.

The wonder of such an idea made her catch her breath. And, even if it were to prove a brief interlude, she knew that if he continued to make the right moves, if he were to drift kisses the length of her throat as he was doing now, nothing, nothing in the world would stop her…

Then they were in the bedroom—and she with no very clear idea of how they had got there. But her top had parted from the waistband of her skirt and his hand caressed, slipped seductively over the black satin underskirt she had chosen, by sheer joyful chance, to wear today for the first time. And now she determined he must see it. And admire.

Casually, as if she were used to such situations, she detached herself, released the catch on her skirt and allowed it to spill onto the floor. He was watching with a half-smile which she rewarded by leaning forward, putting her mouth to his and parting her lips provocatively, before straightening up.

One smooth elegant move and she had pulled the polo over her head—making, of course, a complete mess of her hair, but that mattered to neither of them, since his attention was focused entirely on her face. Like hers, his breathing was excited—more so when he took in the brief, low-cut black lace, the barely covered expanse of creamy skin. His hand came out to trace the soft, feminine curve; her shudder caused a strap to slip from her shoulder.

'Jake, I...' Suddenly she was nervous, overcome with self-doubt. How could she have imagined that she, inexperienced, would be able to please such a man? But even as that thought registered her hands were reaching out and she was pulling at his tie, sweeping the jacket from his shoulders.

And he was offering his wrists, silently but with a dash of mocking laughter, inviting her assistance with the heavy gold cufflinks. At last her shaking fingers dealt with the task and she leaned forward, eyes closed, to press her cheek to the warm, silky skin.

Opening her lips to taste, to kiss, it was sheer delight to hear him groan and to hear—and ignore, as she knew she was meant to—his meaningless protests. She allowed herself to be pulled onto the bed...

When she woke the sun was casting long shadows, gilding the dark shape of the man who lay beside her, his breathing now settled to a quiet, even rhythm. Her mouth curved into a smile of recollection. She had an urge to lean over, to touch her lips to his so the whole delirious sequence could begin again, those long languorous moments ending in such a wild explosion of sensation...

An unwelcome thought intruded which made her expression grow more sober. By all the rules of her own standards she ought to be suffering the uncomfortable pangs of guilt and remorse, having knowingly made love to a man who was about to be married to someone else. But she couldn't whip up any such feelings, not when she had been so mad for the man since that very first sight.

That, she assured herself seriously, was what had made her fall in a heap at his feet. Not the lack of food or the long flight, not even the excitement of the occasion. It had had nothing to do with any of those. It had been the sight of the man she would love to the end of her life, except...

A tiny cold hand clutched at her heart...

The man lying beside her stirred, sighed. She held her breath. She was trying to force herself to make a move, for if she waited here much longer then there was little doubt...

But, before she could make up her mind, an arm came out, circled her waist and, ignoring her startled gasp, pulled her down and into close contact. The eyes which had been observing her covertly swept open, startling her afresh with their beauty. He smiled—that slow, sensuous expression defeating any idea she might have had that it was time to...'

His hands were measuring her waist span, his eyes

absorbing details of her tangled hair, her tender mouth. 'Don't you feel the slightest bit ashamed?'

'Ashamed?' Her eyes widened in surprise. It was so close to her feelings of a moment before…

'Ashamed—of all those…perhaps not lies, but half-truths you have been feeding me since we first met?' He nuzzled against her cheek and she felt the beginnings of that irresistible upward spiral of delight. Her breathing quickened. 'Ashamed of driving me crazy with jealousy?'

Suspecting the direction of his query, she chose a diversion. 'Where did they come from?' Her finger touched the long dark lashes. 'If you give me a satisfactory answer then I'll think of answering *your* question.'

His mouth was soft and tender against hers; he was laughing, frowning. 'Where did what come from?'

'Those eyes.' Again her finger teased the silky lashes. 'I know Marion's are blue, but these are something else, and since…'

'From my mother, I believe. She was Marion's cousin and they were rather alike, but since I know nothing of my father… My mother never did tell anyone his name. It's even possible she wasn't entirely sure herself. It was that era—flower power, anti-war demos…but for her it all ended too soon. She drowned when I was six months old. Marion and Hugo adopted me, and I couldn't have had better parents.'

'I see.'

'And now that I've answered your questions, what about mine?'

'Which was?' Pretty certain she knew the answer, she struggled to damp down this silly inclination to blush like a schoolgirl.

'You let me think there had been other men— whereas—' his arm pulled her closer into the curve of his body '—I could so easily have hurt you.'

She sighed against his mouth. 'I promise you didn't. Besides—' she gurgled with amusement '—somehow it didn't seem the right moment to impart that particular piece of information. Even if it had come into my mind.'

'Mmm,' he half agreed. 'I can see how you might have thought so, but...'

'But nothing.' Overtaken by a strange kind of yearning she spoke as much to convince herself as Jake. 'Anyway, I shall never regret it, no matter what happens. You must accept that.'

'I do accept it.' Idly his hand stroked her upper arm, stirring the delicate hair follicles. 'And equally you must accept that I did not mean this to happen, Ginny. I didn't have it all planned when I suggested lunch.'

'No.' She bit her lip quite savagely. She knew he was hinting at his marriage plans. At least one of them had a conscience! 'I can see that.' And she, poor fool, had assured herself such a short time ago that she would settle for this...that what happened between them today would last for the rest of her life... Pain tore at her but she strove to speak evenly. 'I suppose I'm as much at fault as you are...'

'Only in that you are so irresistible. If I hadn't seen you dashing along in that dazzling pink coat...'

How could he be facetious when it was her happiness at stake? Her life, almost. Her voice hardly shook. 'After all, I did know you were about to marry…'

'Yes. But only if you'll have me, Ginny.'

'But how can you?' She was so involved with her own misery, she didn't absorb what had been said, allowed accusation to colour her tone. 'That's what I find so hard… How can you want to marry one person and jump into bed with another?' Aware that her control was slipping, she could do little to retrieve it.

'Ginny, my darling…' He was laughing. Laughing! Had even found a hankie for the tears which, to her mortification, were running down her cheeks. 'Are you listening to me? I know the circumstances are not what I planned—the only excuse I can offer is that you have been so frustratingly elusive. But I'm asking, humbly and contritely, if you will marry me as soon as it can be arranged?'

'Wh—what?' The trickle of tears had stopped but her expression was blank. 'What did you say, Jake?'

'You know…' He pursed his lips. 'Your mascara is running, your nose is shiny and I've never fancied weepy women, so I hope you'll answer in the affirmative before I have second thoughts.

'Listen, Ginny, I love you. To distraction I love you. And I'm asking—no, dammit—I'm ordering you to marry me. This evening, if it can be arranged.'

'No, that's not possible.' The legal tone was automatic. 'But—oh, Jake, I thought…' She had thought Bonnie White. But now her mind was on another pos-

sible objection, one he picked up and instantly swept
aside.

'And if you're worrying about Hugo and Marion,
then don't.' He traced the curve of her cheek with a
distracting finger. 'You see, when I was summoned
to Singapore it was so I could be told of your relationship with Hugo. He had found it was something
he couldn't keep from Marion, and when she had recovered from the shock he put it to her—and she
agreed—that you and I might not be indifferent to
each other. And in that case...

'It didn't take them long to realise that any possible
attraction we felt was bound to be doomed if you were
under the impression that I was your half-brother.'

'Oh, all this must have been a bolt from the blue
for your mother! I ought not to have let things run
out of control the way they did...'

'Now—what *was* it you said a moment ago about
regrets?' His frown as he loomed over her was light-
hearted. 'I hope you're not having those at this stage
in our relationship.'

'No.' Her head moved against the pillow in a negative gesture. 'No, I'm not having regrets.' Her mouth
moved against his, her lips parted and there was a
long silence as his arm beneath her waist tightened,
pulling her body into a more positive contact with his.

'But...' As he spoke she reached up, touching the
excited pulse in his throat. He caught her fingers before continuing. 'I'm still waiting for an answer to
that important question I asked just a few minutes
ago...'

'And that was?' She appeared to frown with the

effort of recollection, relishing the opportunity to tease.

'That was—' his arm tightened menacingly '—as you know very well...how soon will you marry me?'

'Oh, Jake, are you sure it's going to be as simple as all that? I can't imagine how your parents will react.'

'I think they'll be delighted. For us and for themselves. I'm pretty sure Mother had you marked down as a prospective daughter-in-law right from the beginning. Besides, it is a decision for us in the end...'

'Yes, but they are so kind—I should hate to be the cause of dissension. Maybe...' she hesitated. 'Maybe it would be best to go on like this for the time being, let them become used to the idea...'

'I don't think that would work. You see, I can't bear the idea of being apart from you for any length of time and, even more, an affair is not what I want with you. I meant it when I said I didn't plan to get you into bed right away.' Her sceptically raised eyebrow made him grin. 'And *don't* ask me if I have regrets, for I shall plead the Fifth Amendment.'

'So, you're positive your parents would have no objection?' Her tone remained unconvinced.

'I promise you. My mother has long since run out of eligible young women...'

'Mmm. Eligible. That's what I mean.'

'And you, I promise, are the most eligible she could possibly imagine.' Seeing she was about to interrupt he put a finger over her lips. 'Simply because I love you so.'

'Oh, Jake...' A hand snaked about his neck, pulling

his face close to hers. 'And I love you…so desperately.'

'Then say it for heaven's sake,' he challenged, refusing to allow himself to be diverted. 'I swear that
this could amount to mental cruelty. Repeat after me,
"I love you, Jake Vanbrugh, and I promise to marry
you as soon as it can be arranged."'

'I love you.' How sweet it was to give in, to be so
unusually submissive. 'I love you, Jake Vanbrugh,
and I promise to marry you just as soon as it can be
arranged. Within reason, that is.'

'Now, don't spoil things.' His mouth brushed
against hers. 'I was so enjoying listening to that meek,
humble tone.'

'If that is the kind of wife you think you'll be getting…'

'I don't. I have few illusions.'

'Then you ought to have proposed to someone else,
in fact.' It was impossible to resist a tiny dig. 'When
Mr Welsh said you were to be married, the first person
who came into my mind was Bonnie White.'

'Really? I wonder why.' With his fingers tracing
across tender, excited skin it wasn't easy for her to
remember what they were discussing. 'I suppose,' he
went on lazily, 'because she's so pretty and…
young… Oh, and she's heiress to one of the largest
spreads in the whole of Virginia. Mmm, I wonder why
I didn't think of that before? I suppose it's too late
now.'

'Much…much too late.' Feeling so secure, it was
easy for her to smile—but had he put these points just

a few hours earlier, she knew she would have been devastated by misery and sheer jealousy.

'Well, I shall have to try to live with that.' A curious little smile flitted across his face. At her enquiringly raised eyebrow it became a blatant grin.

'What…what are you thinking, Jake Vanbrugh?'

'I was simply remembering that night when we got home after dancing at the country club…'

'Mmm.' She felt the colour rise in her cheeks and tried to wriggle deeper under the bedclothes, but she was thwarted, and gave up the struggle when his fingers circled her throat.

'Remembering how very fetching you looked wearing nothing but a dark choker round your neck.'

'Oh.' She could think of nothing to say to that.

'And I'm wondering if you ever wear it in bed, by any chance.'

For a moment her brain refused to function, but when it did she had to struggle to maintain an impassive expression. 'Frequently, but only on the most auspicious occasions. If I had known you had bed in mind I should have brought it with me. But you said, quite distinctly, you were taking me to lunch.'

He grinned at the clever way she had turned the tables. 'And I suppose what you're saying is that, since I fell down on that, you are hungry.'

'I'm starving.' Sighing, she trailed a finger down his arm. 'I've heard so often about men like you, who promise lunch when they mean bed.'

'Yeah.' A soft throaty chuckle. 'Can't believe my luck. And now I'm going to be even more shameless and invite you to join me in the shower.'

'Jake.' Her eyes widened in assumed dismay. 'As I told you once before, don't rush me—though…' she gave a wry grin as the eyes sparkled up at him '…look where that got me.' With a lithe wriggle she slid lower in the bed and linked her arms more persuasively about his neck.

'I'm looking,' he said as he did exactly that, laughing aloud when she blushed. 'And you give the distinct impression of asking for more.'

'I wonder what makes you think that?' Reaching up, she brushed her mouth across his.

'Oh, just one or two things.'

'Jake…' She sighed as his fingers trailed across her skin. And again as his hand slipped beneath her, raising her into closer contact.

'So long as you realise this is the last time before I take you off to Virginia and marry you…'

'Virginia?' Her eyes flicked open for a split second before the eyelids dropped again. 'Married in Virginia.' Then she gave a tiny giggle, as if she were surprising herself. 'Whatever you want Jake.' And they began the tender, wanton teasing game which drove everything from her mind.

CHAPTER TEN

THREE weeks later, standing in front of the glass in her bedroom in Virginia, Ginny still found it hard to believe it had all happened. That in such a short time she had tendered her resignation, severing all connection with the firm where she had intended to pursue her long-term career, and had begun tentative enquiries about putting the flat on the market, should Kate find it impossible to raise a mortgage. That and a hundred other things made it amazing that she had ever caught the flight Jake had insisted on booking for her.

Her life had moved not just into top gear but into overdrive—so fast that her recollection was blurred and indistinct, so exhausting that, when she had arrived the previous day, Marion had taken one look and ordered her to bed. There she had slept for fourteen hours, waking once to sip some tea and totter to the bathroom before drifting back into blissful, restorative sleep.

But now, fully refreshed, Ginny felt ready to face the ordeal waiting for her downstairs. After a critical examination of her reflection she was confident she would not let Jake down. Nor Marion. Nor Hugo.

They had been so wonderfully kind and understanding when she had met them again. Both coping, with every appearance of enthusiasm, with the large reception this evening as well as the arrangements for the smaller, much more intimate wedding in two days' time.

A firm knock at the door sent her whirling round in a rustle of silk, eyes and mouth smiling as Jake appeared, closing the door behind him.

'You look like some wonderfully exotic butterfly.' His expression was, like the tone of his voice, a caress. Her heart began to beat loudly...they mustn't...she mustn't... Not with dozens of guests due to arrive. But it was so difficult when they had had barely a moment together since London...

'You like it?' How sensible to concentrate on the dress, to be diverted by it. But her question was a formality, since she knew she was looking pretty special. She moved, demonstrating the flow of the skirt, her eyes full of flirtatious appeal. 'You don't think it's too...?'

'It is "too"...' He grinned. 'Much too much "too"... The pity of it is that Mother is waiting in the hall—but for that, I swear... But just think...two days and we shall be away from all this. And before we go down...' A tiny box emerged from his pocket, to reveal a solitaire diamond, on a narrow platinum band, flashing fire...

'Oh, Jake...' She caught her breath. 'It's quite, quite perfect.' And it was. When he slipped it onto the slender pink-tipped finger it might have been made for her hand. 'Thank you.' And, standing on tiptoe, she pulled his head down to hers, breathing in the astringent fragrance of him as their mouths touched.

'I suppose…' His voice was husky, humorous. 'I suppose I can't persuade you to let me stay with you now, to forget what is happening downstairs and…?'

'I would,' she said mischievously, 'but I don't want you to break that promise you made in London.'

'Ah. I was hoping you might have forgotten.'

'No chance.'

'I can't imagine why I ever made such a stupid, completely frustrating commitment… But, if that's your last word, then I suggest the only thing we can do is go down. But—one last look…'

Fingers entwined, they stood in front of the glass—he tall, impressive as ever, in dark tuxedo, with brilliant white shirt, and she in the soft red cashmere, which suited her amazingly, clung lovingly to the full curves, emphasised the slender waist. At the back it was slashed into a wide inverted V, leaving an expanse of smooth skin. She wriggled as Jake's fingers explored each bone in her spine. The skirt was an extravaganza—full, and swaying from a deep cummerbund, the sheen and rustle of the silk adding excitement to beauty.

Walking downstairs with Jake, the skirt slightly raised, the diamond glittering on her finger, his touch on her elbow giving her confidence, Ginny felt more like a heroine from some period drama, than the modern, emancipated female from London she knew herself to be. Acting like an old-fashioned girl, she admitted with a sly sideways glance at Jake who, intercepting it, raised an enquiring eyebrow.

'Nothing.' Her eyes gleamed in self-satisfied innocence. They reached the hall as Marion and Hugo came towards them. 'At least, nothing I'm prepared to confess right now.'

That secret smile kept coming and going as she stood in the receiving line, automatically replying to good wishes as guests arrived. For how could she admit that the instant he had snapped his fingers, she had come running? All previous views on equality simply abandoned—career, home, friends, all tossed out of the window... Who would have thought it? And yet...she felt not the hint of a doubt, not a trace of uncertainty...

In a kind of dream she drifted through the evening—dancing, when the music began, with the man she would marry so soon. Their eyes were on each other, oblivious of the crowd of friends who smiled and clapped as they circled the room, her skirt floating about her in the most romantic way possible.

And then, later, Jake whispered something in her ear, hurrying her through one of the French windows out onto the terrace and along the shadowy side of the house to a waiting car.

'What...?' She was breathless with excitement and emotion. 'Where are we going, Jake?' Carefully he swept her skirts inside and came round to the driver's seat without answering. 'It seems so rude...'

'I have a surprise for you—and we shall be back before anyone realises we're missing. Mother knows where we're going, so don't worry.' A quick kiss was dropped on her forehead before he started the engine and a few moments later they were pulling up outside the stables, where a grinning Miguel was waiting to open her door.

'Careful, now, you mustn't damage that beautiful skirt.' Jake took her hand to lead her across the immaculate paving to one of the stables where a light gleamed through the open half-door. 'But I wanted you to see what arrived yesterday.'

They leaned over the top, where they had a perfect view of the tiny foal snuffling against his mother's flank.

'Oh, Jake. How wonderful.' She held out her hand and the chestnut mare nuzzled softly at her fingertips. The foal was much darker than his mother but with a chestnut mane and tail. 'And you say he was born yesterday?'

'Yes, on the very day you came back to Virginia. And it's a she. She is Randy's daughter.'

'Oh…' The tiny foal came over, put her tender mouth to Ginny's hand before turning in search of her mother. 'So incredibly gentle.'

'And she's for you. My present to you, so we shall always remember the day you came to me.'

'Jake.' Tears stung at her eyes. Her mind was filled with so many thoughts and memories, such a mixture of pain and delight, so many conflicting impressions. 'You really want to give me Randy's foal? His last one? When he meant so much to you?'

Jake didn't at once reply, but they stood there in the stable yard, looking at each other. His dark eyes had a passionate intensity. 'Don't you know, it's because he meant so much to me that I want you to have her?' Passion blazed unquenched between them, but when, after a moment, he bent his head, his kiss was cool, deliberately chaste. His voice was neither of those. 'But now maybe we ought to go back to our guests. While we can.'

The wedding day dawned fine—as perfect an autumn day, according to Martha, when she brought breakfast trays for Ginny and Kate, as Virginia was likely to produce even for a Vanbrugh wedding. A twitch of the curtain had proved her point as she'd gestured towards the bank of trees in every shade of gold, glorious and dramatic against a pale blue morning sky.

'Mmm.' Yawning, Kate pushed herself upright in her bed, reached for her napkin and spooned a sliver of melon into her mouth. 'Mmm,' she said again, this time with approval.

'I suppose you're still tired after the flight yesterday—but bless you, Kate, for making the effort.'

'Oh, it was no effort I assure you, love. Especially when I was presented with my ticket. Only...' She gave a tiny sigh. 'I'm not sure I was *wise* to come.'

'Oh?' Startled, Ginny paused in the act of pouring coffee, glancing across at the other bed. 'What on earth do you mean, Kate?'

'Simply that I'm going to have to go back to London and all that entails—to the demands of an alarm clock and an exacting boss—and I'll be remembering you, with breakfast trays being brought up by the devoted Martha. It's more than enough to drive anyone mad with jealousy.'

'Ah.' Ginny grinned. 'Is that all? Then let me reassure you. Jake and I are going to live in his flat in New York so we'll be on our own. No Martha at our beck and call...'

'But a lady of leisure nonetheless.'

'Not that either. You see, I've decided I'd better go back to law school to try to bridge the gap between the two systems. I don't want to abandon my career potential.'

'I see…' Kate finished her fruit, poured some tea, and began nibbling on toast and preserve. 'I didn't think you'd be considering a career, not when you're marrying into such a wealthy family.'

'I'm not saying I shall, but it would be good to have a choice. I refuse to let all that skill simply atrophy. That would break my heart after so many years of hard slog.'

'What does Jake think?'

'Jake wants me to do what I think right.'

'So long as what you want doesn't take you away from him?' her friend judged.

'Something like that.' Ginny laughed, not minding the colour touching her cheek. 'That would suit us both.'

'Mmm. Not hard to see the man adores you. Lucky Ginny.'

'Yes, I do know how lucky I am.' She owed so much to the Vanbrughs that she would never be able to repay.

Kate interrupted her thoughts just a touch diffidently. 'Are you feeling nervous, Ginny? Not just about the wedding, but, you know, taking the plunge—committing yourself?'

'A bit, I guess.' But not in the way Kate meant. Her colour deepened again, though she wasn't about to make any confessions. 'Excited, but with no doubts whatsoever.'

'That I can appreciate, and it would be hard to understand if you said anything else. Not when you've nabbed the dreamiest man I've seen in years, and not when he has rich and charming parents who are almost as keen on you as he is, and...'

'I admit everything, Kate, and I still can't believe my luck.'

'Well...' Kate considered. 'That's not to say he isn't lucky too. I just wish I had seen him first, though I doubt if he would have noticed. I don't suppose well-built redheads are his cup of tea...'

'Well built!' Ginny scoffed. 'I just wish you would forget this phobia about weight—you must know you have the kind of figure men love...'

'Yeah, Rubens and Edward the Seventh—but they aren't round these days...'

'And if they were you wouldn't fancy them. But, incidentally, Jake's best man—whom I haven't met so far—is, I understand, very eligible. He's two years older than Jake and he might even be looking for a wife. He ought to be arriving within the next hour. I hope he won't be late, or—'

'Well, speaking of that—' With a determined move Kate rose and placed her tray on a stool '—I suppose it is one of my duties to make sure the bride is on time, so how would it be if I were to use the bathroom first? Then you'll be able to take your time, beautify yourself before getting into your glad rags...'

'Fine. Oh, and Kate, don't forget, a hairdresser is

due later on, so take your time in the bath and I shall just have ten minutes' shut-eye.'

'I'm actually beginning to feel rather excited.' Kate, still wearing her dressing-gown, was on her knees on the carpet twitching the hem of Ginny's gown. She looked up with a smile. 'All those weddings I've been to and this is the first time I've felt even a twinge of excitement.' She got to her feet and viewed the hem critically before deciding it was as it should be. 'Must be something to do with being in Virginia. Oh, Ginny, you look… I hope ''ravishing'' isn't too indelicate a word in the circumstances.'

'Mmm.' The nervy giggle faded to a half-smile as she turned to her reflection. Disagreement would have been hypocritical, but even at this late stage she would not risk tempting fate. 'Fine feathers!' she dismissed lightly, while deep down there was a grateful acknowledgement that the dress, bought in such haste in London, could hardly have been improved.

Pale cream duchess satin, it had a scooped neckline edged with pearls, a skirt narrow in front with the slight suggestion of a train behind, and long tight sleeves.

The hairdresser had insisted her hair was quite long enough for a chignon—a style which looked wonderful with the spray of cream roses holding the elbow-length veil in position. And she held the posy of flowers which had just arrived from Jake—roses and orchids in a cloudy haze of baby's breath fern. It was just exquisite, while the message on the accompanying card…

A tap at the door announced Marion's arrival as Kate, make-up completed, was easing her dress over her head, struggling to reach the zip. 'Let me help you with that.' Quickly Marion completed the task and gave a final twitch to Kate's *eau-de-Nil* gown before standing back, head to one side. 'You both look perfectly lovely.'

As she spoke, her voice not entirely steady, the eyes which met Ginny's in a look of warmth and understanding were particularly brilliant. It was only Kate's presence which held Ginny back from her instinctive wish to show Marion how she felt. After the long talk they had had yesterday so many questions had been answered, and the foundations of a deep relationship had been established.

As a break from the preparations they had decided on a relaxing walk down to the stables, using the new foal as an excuse. But it had immediately become clear that Marion had planned the excursion for a more practical reason. 'You know, Ginny, I don't want you ever to blame Hugo for what happened between him and…and your mother.'

'Oh, but I don't,' she'd said automatically, but not quite truthfully.

'Well, it would be strange if you didn't, my dear.' Slowing her pace as they walked down the sun-dappled avenue, she slipped her hand through Ginny's arm. 'But I want you to know it was my fault at least as much as Hugo's.'

Ginny could think of nothing to say; she still found it difficult to comprehend how a man could deceive a woman like Marion.

'Maybe you find that hard to understand.' Marion sighed. 'Attitudes have changed so much. But, you see, I did let Hugo down. When *we* married a wife was expected to follow her husband—just as he was expected to support her—and I married a soldier. I was *proud* to marry a soldier. I knew exactly what I was doing.

'I meant to have him the first time I met him, at a summer ball at West Point. I meant to be a good wife and make him happy. But then I found I hated army life, and after a while I came back home to live here with my parents, where I'd been born and brought up. I was selfish. I see that now. But at first Hugo didn't mind. He wanted me to be happy, too, and there were so many demands on high-flying officers—always flying off to Washington or to one of our embassies abroad.

'In the meantime I had had it confirmed I'd never be able to have children—that must have made me more difficult still. Even when Hugo came on leave I could hardly lift myself out of depression. I think being able to adopt Jake might have saved my reason— does that seem completely heartless, when it was only by his mother's death...?'

'No. No, I can understand that.'

'But even then I handled it badly. I became an obsessive mother and, though I didn't mean to, I neglected Hugo. We were living apart, he came home only on furlough, and it must have seemed to him I was more interested in the child—someone else's child—than I was in him. A classic situation—and I ought to have had more sense—but there you are. We are none of us as clever as we like to think we are.'

'Well, it's much easier to see things clearly from a distance.'

'Mmm.' Marion sighed as they began to walk the last few hundred yards towards the stable block. 'Anyway, by the time Hugo was posted to Vietnam things between us were distinctly rocky. His last leave had been so strained that even my parents had noticed something was wrong. Afterwards I learned he had gone back three days earlier than he needed, and had gone deep-sea fishing so he could relax. What can I say? Except that to the end of my days I shall regret what happened, and if he had been killed—as he so nearly was—' She shuddered. 'I try not to think of that.'

'Well...' it was Ginny's turn to give a comforting squeeze '—if it makes you feel better I would say you now have a truly happy marriage.'

'Yes, now we have. We have been so fortunate to have a second chance—but it was Hugo's injuries, all those months in a military hospital that mended things for me. I left Jake here with my parents and spent that time near the hospital on the West Coast until I could bring him home. We had lots of time to talk, amid all the pain and trauma. He told me there had been someone else but that it was over. I was so frightened when I thought of life without him...'

'Thank you, Marion, for telling me all this.'

'Oh, and one last thing.' The eyes she turned towards Ginny shone with affection. 'When Hugo told me the truth about who you were it was a shock—it would be silly to deny that—but now I'm positively glad, because I know you're going to make my son very happy.'

'I promise I'm going to do my very best.'

'And that's what I want more than anything in the world.' They stood smiling at each other, both rather emotional. Marion had looked beyond her. 'And now, I think, if you turn round, you'll see him walking along to meet us, so you go on. I'm sure this is one occasion when I shan't be missed. I'll cut across this way—I can see Miguel and I want to have a word with him.'

But that had been yesterday. And today, once again, Marion was offering all the encouragement Ginny would have expected from her own mother. 'You're both ready, then?' Head to one side, she scrutinised them for any tiny flaw, then nodded. 'Quite perfect. Everyone is waiting for you downstairs, and…and Hugo is waiting to give you away, my dear.'

Slowly, with infinite care for the dresses, the little group descended to the hall, where Hugo was ready to join them, and then went through the salon towards the French windows, which were open to the gardens where the guests were seated in the warm midday sunshine.

Ginny could see the clergyman standing waiting for her to walk along the gold-coloured carpet. She could see the tall outline of the man with whom she was about to exchange lifelong vows—and the back of his head, and another dark-clad figure standing beside him.

From somewhere out of sight music began to

play—something so familiar and evocative that into her mind, unbidden, came images of her mother, of Tom, her father… Tears stung and her hand began to shake.

Then it was clasped, steadied by one just as firm, just as sure as Tom's would have been. The tears were blinked away. She turned to give Hugo a little smile of reassurance, saw the relief, the confidence—perhaps even love—in his expression. And certainly, when he spoke, his voice was filled with tenderness and understanding. 'Are you ready now, Virginia?'

'I'm ready.'

She turned for a last exchange with Kate, then they were walking down through the banks of flowers to the soaring music from 'Lohengrin'. And as she reached Jake he turned towards her, his mouth curving slightly upwards, eyes gleaming as they absorbed details of her dress. His hands reached out and his fingers linked with hers, his father having relinquished his claim on the other side.

And then she heard his name as he was invited to make his commitment.

'Hugo Jacob Vanbrugh, do you take Virginia Sophie Browne…?'

The order of the names was reversed and she heard her own voice making the responses with the same firm certainty he had shown.

She knew then it was right—what had happened all those years ago had been ordained, had been meant to lead to this perfect moment. She knew she had come home.

CHAPTER ELEVEN

THE helicopter lifted, causing such a downrush of air that Jake put his arm about her in protection. They waved to the pilot and stood watching a moment longer as the machine rose, diminished and quickly disappeared among the encircling hills before they crossed the verandah of the log cabin which was to be home for the first few days of their married life.

'Jake,' she gasped as he swept her off her feet, shouldered open the door and carried her inside before slowly releasing her, allowing her toes to touch the ground. 'Jake…' Breathless, she shook her head in attempted reproof in the split second before his mouth closed on hers.

'At last…' Cradling her face between his palms, he gazed down soberly before a faint smile curved his lips. 'At last I've got you to myself. I had begun to think this time would never arrive…'

'But, Jake…' Smiling dreamily, she linked her arms about his neck. 'It couldn't possibly have been arranged sooner.' She was enjoying being provocative. 'Even as it is, my feet haven't touched the ground since…since that day in London, and…'

'And speaking of that…'

She gave him another glance of mock reproof. 'And your mother must have been in a flat spin trying to cope with all the arrangements. First the evening reception, then the wedding itself.' Sighing reminiscently, she laid her head on his shoulder. 'It was the most perfect wedding imaginable.'

'Mmm.' The arms around her tightened; she felt his mouth move against the crown of her head. 'But that was all down to just one detail—that you were the bride, I the bridegroom. *Ergo* perfection.'

'You liked the dress?' Dreamily she began a review of the perfect day—remembered her pleasure in the dropped-pearl earrings, a twenty-first birthday gift from her grandmother.

She grew serious for a moment. Yes, in all the important aspects she had been her real grandmother, just as Tom had been her true father. And she was confident that neither of them would have stood in the way of her present happiness.

'I loved the dress.' He sounded tolerant, amused, indulgent—exactly, she decided with a touch of self-satisfaction, how a newly married man ought to sound.

'Oh, and Jake—thank you for the lovely flowers. They looked so perfect with the dress.'

'It was a pleasure, my darling.'

'And Kate's dress—' she went on. 'It really suited her, didn't it?'

'Yes, I adored Kate's dress. And my mother's dress. In fact. I loved every single thing about the wedding.'

'And it was so touching when your father said in his speech how much he had always longed for a daughter and now he had one...'

'And you and I know he meant every word.'

'Yes.' Her voice was all at once thick with unshed tears. 'He told me exactly that the previous day. I still have shivers when I think how much of a shock my sudden appearance must have been. At the time he must have wished he'd never heard of me—but now, I do believe, he is happy about it. And I agree with him—it's a secret we shall share, just the four of us.'

'No one else need ever know of it.'

'No. I hope not... Oh, did I tell you about my compliment from the Colonel? He told me I had the definite look of an actress he used to know.'

'Well, I'm sure he put a few through his hands when he was younger. Did he mention her name?'

'Mmm, but it didn't mean much to me. Oh, it's not important. I'll tell you all about it some other time.'

'I'm just relieved that the parents had some inkling as to how I felt. If they hadn't...'

'Don't!' she implored, with an involuntary shiver which made his arms tighten as if a threat still existed.

'But if it hadn't been for Mother's intuition they might never have shared your secret with me—would never have seen the need.'

'So many if's. If it hadn't been for the whole sequence of events, I would not have come to New York in the first place—most certainly I would not have bluffed my way into your offices, past the formidable Karen Lavery.'

That brought a faint smile to his face, but then it faded. 'When I had that call from Mother, asking me to fly out to Singapore, I can't tell you what I imagined. I suppose I was feeling pretty low already—

wanting to follow you to London, afraid of another brush-off.'

'I'm sure you must have spent your whole adult life being afraid of a brush-off from one woman or another,' she mocked, brushing her mouth against his.

'From you.' He corrected. 'I said nothing about anyone else. Anyway, I flew out to the parents not knowing quite what I'd find, and certainly with no idea that any of it involved you. Then, when I reached Raffles Hotel—where they were spending a night or two—and when they told me... For a while I simply could not take it in. Suddenly...a blinding light. Was it possible that this was why, with all the signals pointing in one direction, you'd so assiduously rejected each of my tentative advances...?'

'Tentative!' Ginny exploded.

'You yourself mentioned a casual goodnight kiss.'

But that was a reminder she chose to ignore. 'Tentative? When after we had been to the club you had me on the bed? Can you begin to imagine how I would have felt if I hadn't come to my senses? If events had been allowed to reach a natural conclusion?'

'And speaking of that...' A trail of light, heady kisses touched her cheek, came to a teasing halt at one side of her mouth. 'Would you like to see the bedroom?'

'In a moment.' Indulging in light-hearted teasing was surprisingly exciting.

'Thwarted again.' The brilliant eyes smiled down in complicity. 'Just like in London. When I arrived at your flat ready to be swept off my feet... No, don't laugh. I promise you, I was ready and eager—and that was when you produced that feeble…Nick, wasn't it?'

'Mmm. Kate's brother,' she agreed dreamily. 'Oh, and Jake, Kate was thrilled with the bracelet you gave her.'

'I thought attorneys were trained to stick to the subject.'

'I just thought you would like to know. Anyway, we've been all through the Nick connection already, but if anyone had told me—' She paused, shaking her head in mild disbelief.

'Go on.' Nudging her gently with his chin, he had the chance to study her expression closely. 'If anyone had told you…?'

'If anyone had suggested I'd meet someone and abandon everything and follow him to the ends of the earth and marry him within a month or two…'

'The ends of the earth, eh?' Eyes gleamed threateningly. 'As I told you once before, most Virginians would be deeply offended by such a description—especially since they know their State is just about the centre of the universe.'

She glanced around, one eyebrow raised questioningly. 'But Virginians are more than a little inclined to exaggerate. At least, if this is what they call a log cabin.'

'It *is* built entirely of wood.'

'Mmm. But not of logs, I suggest.' She rubbed the toe of a patent shoe on the immaculately smooth polished floor.

'Once upon a time it *was* a simple log cabin—the family rebuilt it about twenty, thirty years ago.'

'And now it's a luxury holiday home.'

'Something like that. The parents come when they feel the need to get away, to unwind completely. And when someone had the bright idea that we spend our first few days here, I thought…' He hesitated.

'Yes?' She raised luminous brown eyes and when she interpreted his expression felt herself begin to blush. 'Yes? You thought…what?'

He was laughing. 'I thought about it in great detail—in fact, I would go so far as to say I thought of little else. I planned everything and plotted. I planned to woo you—after all, I hadn't had the chance to do a great deal of that. So I decided I'd woo you with the most delicious meal, ply you with the finest wines, and then…'

'Hmm?' The blush was dying, and a smile curved her mouth as she flicked him an upward glance—a consciously provocative, flirtatious glance. 'And then?'

'And then I meant to take you to bed and make love to you till you begged for mercy. But now…'

'But what about that other promise—you said you'd show me the Blue Ridge Mountains.'

'Ah. Those. Well, I promise there's the most perfect view of them from the bedroom window—from the bed itself, if you'd care to look.'

'Remember how once I asked you not to crowd me…?' In apparent abstraction she rubbed her cheek against his.

'Mmm. I do remember. But if you mean to repeat the instruction, you are unlikely to find me so tolerant.'

Wide-eyed she looked up at him. 'Promise?'

For a moment he stared, before resigning himself to a wave of delighted amusement. 'You minx.' His eyes darkened as he gazed down at her, his thumbs caressing the planes of her face as the smile gradually faded.

'I am *so* looking forward to being married to you.' As she was about to interrupt, his fingers across her mouth stopped her. '*And* I don't simply mean in the way you are thinking, but as I was about to explain to you earlier... Now where was I? I seem unable to keep my mind on what I'm saying when you look at me with that peculiar expression...'

'Peculiar?' Her tone was loud with outrage.

'Peculiarly sensual...arousing. And that is something you ought to address soon.' His eyes sparkled with mischief, especially when he saw the colour rise in her cheeks.

'You *were* going to tell me something.' With an effort she was able to maintain an appearance of detachment.

'Ah, yes.' He seemed unable to wrench his eyes from hers—a problem they had in common, Ginny reflected in a moment's detachment. 'I was describing how I'd planned to wine and dine you, then to carry you off to...' Laughter gurgled in his voice. 'To admire the Blue Ridge Mountains, but now... I think if we were to do things in reverse order...'

For a second she couldn't follow his drift, but the moment she did it was clear she approved. 'Ah, and since it seems no time at all since we were eating that delicious wedding breakfast...'

There was no need to say any more for they were already moving, without the least suggestion of haste, taking time to kiss, to tease and to sigh, revelling in the tantalising build-up, in the heightened sense of touch, of taste, in the novelty and delight of exploration.

Only when they reached the bedroom was Ginny briefly diverted—firstly by the sun slanting in through the window, deepening the already glowing shades of wood on wall and floor, and then by the striking patchwork quilts, one covering the bed and a second, even more beautiful, the single decoration on the wall above.

'Oh, Jake.' She had no need to explain her distraction, the direction of her interest was obvious.

'The one on the wall is two hundred years old—it's called "Kentucky Rose" and it was stitched by Mother's several times great-grandmother. The one on the bed is called "Wedding Ring", and it's supposed to ensure fertility for those who sleep beneath it. So...don't you think this is the most appropriate moment to put it to the test?'

'Oh, Jake!' Again she felt her skin grow hot, but she was laughing, linking her arms about his neck and not resisting when they collapsed onto the bed—nor when he began to unfasten the row of tiny buttons on her butter-yellow blouse. She abetted when he began to pull the pins from her hair, rejoicing in the touch which pushed delicate straps from her shoulders and traced heady, sensuous paths across her skin. Never, never would she resist.

When he spoke, his voice was low and husky as he

pushed her deeper into the incredible softness of the pillows. 'Do you remember that very first evening, when I made a forecast which you contradicted fiercely? Do you remember?' he insisted as she reached up, twining her fingers through his hair.

'No.' How could she think, remember, when those bewildering eyes, more violet-blue than in her wildest dreams, were gazing down with that entrancing mix of mischief and purpose? When his hands... Ginny held her breath for a delicious, shuddering moment. 'No, I don't.'

'I told you you would be married within two years. And your reaction was total rejection—with a hint of misogamy.'

'No.' She smiled. 'Never that. Perhaps if I had known you were putting yourself forward as a candidate...'

'Oh?' His mouth was very close to hers. 'In that case, I was at fault for failing to make my position clear. And since we have wasted so much time...'

It was early evening when she woke. All that remained of the day was a streak of rose-gold in the sky, the dark hills in stark relief.

'Tea?' Jake, a brief towel round his waist, came into the room with two cups on a tray, one of which he put on the table beside her. He smiled, shaking his head in reproof as she tried to pull a cover up to her chin. 'It's too late for that.' Perching on the bed, he leaned forward, rubbing his cheek on hers. 'Much too late for modesty. And don't, please don't, tell me you're sorry.'

'Much too late for that too,' she teased, then grew more serious. 'But I'm not. How could I be, when...?' Fingers trailing across his naked chest, she caught her breath when she picked up his strong heartbeat. 'When I feel like this?'

'When we both feel like this,' he said huskily as he stretched out beside her, holding her close as they gazed at the darkening sky.

It was a moment before Ginny spoke. Then she whispered, 'Bliss.' Her manner was dreamy. 'Or Joy. Oh, Jake, don't you think so?'

'Both.' Now he was looming over her with that purposeful air, the one which made her heartbeats quicken, encouraged her to wriggle a little lower in the bed. 'Yes, definitely both.' And he was laughing.

'Not *that*.' Meaning to be repressive, instead she sounded soft and yielding and seductive. 'I was thinking about the foal—you said I should choose a name which would remind us...'

His mouth brushed against hers. 'Then let's try them out again. It would be a pity if we found we had made the wrong choice after all.'

'Mmm.' To disagree would have been perverse, since it was a plan she approved wholeheartedly. And it would have been impossible when he was doing that...and that... But she was certain their decision was about to be made...it was...Bliss.

MILLS & BOON®

Next Month's Romances

Each month you can choose from a wide variety of romance novels from Mills & Boon. Below are the new titles to look out for next month from the Presents™ and Enchanted™ series.

Presents™

Enchanted™

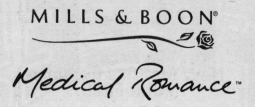

MILLS & BOON®

Medical Romance™

Don't miss Josie Metcalfe's wonderfully heartwarming trilogy...

St Augustine's Hospital

We know you'll love getting to know this fascinating group of friends

FIRST THINGS FIRST
Nick and Polly's story
in October

SECOND CHANCE
Wolff and Laura's story
in November

THIRD TIME LUCKY
Leo and Hannah's story
in January

St Augustine's: where love surprises everyone

FOUR FREE
specially selected
Enchanted™ novels
PLUS a FREE Mystery Gift
when you return this page...

Return this coupon and we'll send you 4 Mills & Boon® Enchanted™ novels and a mystery gift absolutely FREE! We'll even pay the postage and packing for you.

We're making you this offer to introduce you to the benefits of the Reader Service™– FREE home delivery of brand-new Mills & Boon Enchanted novels, at least a month before they are available in the shops, FREE gifts and a monthly Newsletter packed with information, competitions, author profiles and lots more...

Accepting these FREE books and gift places you under no obligation to buy, you may cancel at any time, even after receiving just your free shipment. Simply complete the coupon below and send it to:

MILLS & BOON READER SERVICE, FREEPOST, CROYDON, SURREY, CR9 3WZ.

READERS IN EIRE PLEASE SEND COUPON TO PO BOX 4546, DUBLIN 24

NO STAMP NEEDED

Yes, please send me 4 free Enchanted novels and a mystery gift. I understand that unless you hear from me, I will receive 6 superb new titles every month for just £2.20* each, postage and packing free. I am under no obligation to purchase any books and I may cancel or suspend my subscription at any time, but the free books and gift will be mine to keep in any case.

(I am over 18 years of age)

N7YE

Ms/Mrs/Miss/Mr_____
BLOCK CAPS PLEASE

Address_____

_____

_____ Postcode _____

CAROLE MORTIMER

Gypsy

She'd always been his one temptation...

Shay Flannagan was the raven-haired beauty
the Falconer brothers called Gypsy. They
each found her irresistible, but it was Lyon
Falconer who claimed her—when he didn't
have the right—and sealed her fate.

Meet
A PERFECT FAMILY

Shocking revelations and heartache lie just beneath the surface of their charmed lives.

The Crightons are a family in conflict. Long-held resentments and jealousies are reawakened when three generations gather for a special celebration.

One revelation leads to another - a secret war-time liaison, a carefully concealed embezzlement scam, the illicit seduction of another's wife. The façade begins to crack, revealing a family far from perfect, underneath.

"Women everywhere will find pieces of themselves in Jordan's characters"
–Publishers Weekly

The coupon is valid only in the UK and Eire against purchases made in retail outlets and not in conjunction with any Reader Service or other offer.

50p OFF
COUPON
VALID UNTIL: 31.12.1997
PENNY JORDAN'S *A PERFECT FAMILY*

9 904170 210508 >

0472 00195